The Big Chihuahua

D0556620

Also by Waverly Curtis

Dial C for Chihuahua

Chihuahua Confidential

Published by Kensington Publishing Corporation

TAIL-WAGGING PRAISE FOR THE BARKING DETECTIVE MYSTERIES

CHIHUAHUA CONFIDENTIAL

"Hollywood is the stage for this enjoyable caper starring amateur P.I. Geri Sullivan and her talking Chihuahua/partner, Pepe. The characters are comical, especially Pepe, who will have you laughing out loud. A great read."

    —*RT Book Reviews*, **4 stars**

"Light as a feather and a whole lot of fun."

    —*Seattle Times*

"Hop on board the TV-studio tour bus for this light cozy."

    —*Library Journal*

DIAL C FOR CHIHUAHUA

"Three woofs and a big bow-wow for *Dial C for Chihuahua*. Pepe is one cool sleuth—just don't call him a dog! I really loved the book."

    —**Leslie Meier**, author of the Lucy Stone mysteries

"Readers will sit up and beg for more."

    —**Sushi the Shih Tzu**, canine star of the *Trash 'n' Treasures* mysteries by Barbara Allan

"Writing duo Curtis has created a humorous but deadly serious mystery. Pepe is a delight and more intelligent than most humans in the book. An ex-husband and current love interest keep Geri's life hopping. Crafty plotting will keep you engrossed until the end and have you eagerly awaiting the next book."

    —*RT Book Reviews*, **4 stars**

"Every dog has its day and there'll be plenty of days for Geri Sullivan and Pepe in this fun twist on the typical PI partnership."

—**Simon Wood**, author of *Did Not Finish*

"Waverly Curtis has created a delightful cast of human and canine characters in *Dial C for Chihuahua*. Pepe never loses his essential dogginess, even as he amazes gutsy Geri Sullivan, his partner in crime detection, with his past exploits and keen nose for detail. I look forward to Pepe's next adventure!"

—**Bernadette Pajer**, author of the Professor
Bradshaw Mysteries

"Move over, Scooby-Doo, there's a new dog in town! *Dial C for Chihuahua* is a fun and breezy read, with polished writing and charming characters, both human and canine. If you like a little Chihuahua with your mystery, former purse-dog Pepe is a perfect fit!"

—**Jennie Bentley**, author of the Do-It-Yourself
Home Renovation mysteries

The Big Chihuahua

Waverly Curtis

KENSINGTON PUBLISHING CORP.

http://www.kensingtonbooks.com

KENSINGTON BOOKS are published by

Kensington Publishing Corp.
119 West 40th Street
New York, NY 10018

Copyright © 2013 by Waverly Curtis

All rights reserved. No part of this book may be reproduced
in any form or by any means without the prior written consent
of the Publisher, excepting brief quotes used in reviews.

If you purchased this book without a cover, you should be
aware that this book is stolen property. It was reported as
"unsold and destroyed" to the Publisher and neither the
Author nor the Publisher has received any payment for this
"stripped book."

All Kensington titles, imprints, and distributed lines are
available at special quantity discounts for bulk purchases for
sales promotions, premiums, fund-raising, and educational
or institutional use. Special book excerpts or customized
printings can also be created to fit specific needs. For details,
write or phone the office of the Kensington Special Sales
Manager: Kensington Publishing Corp., 119 West 40th Street,
New York, NY 10018, Attn: Special Sales Department,
Phone: 1-800-221-2647.

Kensington and the K logo Reg. U.S. Pat. & TM Off.

ISBN-13: 978-0-7582-7497-7
ISBN-10: 0-7582-7497-1
First Kensington Mass Market Edition: October 2013

eISBN-13: 978-0-7582-9158-5
eISBN-10: 0-7582-9158-2
First Kensington Electronic Edition: October 2013

10 9 8 7 6 5 4 3 2 1

Printed in the United States of America

Chapter 1

"Do you think our boss will like it?" I asked my dog as I reached into the backseat to grab the framed newspaper clipping.

"It does not matter what I think," said Pepe with a bitter tone in his voice. My small white Chihuahua was sitting in the passenger seat. "I am just a dog."

"Yes, but a dog that talks," I said.

"But, *que lastima*, you are the only one who can hear me," Pepe said. "If only I could have spoken to the reporter, I would have set her straight." He was referring to the story that had been published in the *L.A. Times* about the resolution of our last case. I had cut it out and framed it for our boss, Jimmy Gerrard, who was prominently featured in the article. It downplayed the part Pepe and I had played, which was fine with me. It's pretty hard to explain that your dog talks. But it galled Pepe that he didn't get more credit for taking down the bad guys.

"Maybe we'll have better luck with this new case," I said. "Jimmy G said it's perfect for us."

We had parked right in front of the run-down brick building where Jimmy G has his office. It is on the edge of downtown Seattle in a slightly seedy neighborhood, which suits our boss fine, as he likes to think of himself as a hard-boiled detective of the same ilk as Philip Marlowe.

The building always seems to be empty. I've never run into anyone in the lobby or while walking down the hall, although there are names stenciled on the frosted glass of the doors advertising the offices of a tax preparer, an importing firm, and something called Secret Star Productions. The office of the Gerrard Agency is on the third floor at the end of the hall. There was a letter-sized piece of paper obscuring the familiar gold letters spelling out GERRARD DETECTIVE AGENCY. It had bold red type across the top of it. As I got closer, I saw it was an eviction notice.

"*Que pasa*, Geri?" asked Pepe.

"It says Jimmy G has three days to pay his rent or else he will be kicked out," I said, pulling the paper off the door. I set the framed article down and tried the doorknob, but it was locked. Jimmy G had never given me a key. I rattled the doorknob and knocked on the pane of glass. To help me, Pepe uttered a few of his tiny barks.

"Hey, don't blow a gasket," came a muffled voice from inside. I heard some banging sounds, some shuffling sounds, and then the door opened, revealing a rumpled Jimmy G.

I had always suspected that Jimmy G slept in his office, and his appearance seemed to bear that out. His eyes were bleary and red, and his white shirt was wrinkled. He was still buckling the belt on his tan slacks, and his shoulder holster and gun were hanging on the coat rack by the door, along with his fedora and tan trench coat. He smelled like cheap bourbon and cigar smoke.

He has big brown eyes that are almost as soulful as Pepe's, which may be why I am so tolerant of his bad behavior. He looks like he needs someone to take care of him, which is my weakness. I had adopted Pepe from a local animal shelter when I read about all the Chihuahuas who were being flown up to Seattle from Los Angeles where they were being abandoned in record numbers.

"Look at this!" I said, slapping down the eviction notice on his desk, which was piled high with papers.

"Read it to Jimmy G, doll," he said as he reached into his desk drawer to pull out a bottle of Jim Beam—mostly empty, I noticed. He took a slug, threw back his head and gargled, swallowed, then shook his head like a dog that's wet and said, "Ah, that's better!"

"Well, this is not!" I said. I had totally forgotten about the framed article, which was still outside the door. "It's an eviction notice."

"Oh, Jimmy G thought he heard someone at the door early this morning," he said.

Jimmy G always talked about himself in the third person.

"Well, you have plenty of time to get caught up," I said. "This three-day notice is usually just a warning. As long as you catch up on your rent within three days, they won't proceed with the eviction." I know something about the real estate business because I worked as a stager before the housing market crashed. That's when I applied for and got the job working for Jimmy G. I took it on a lark, thinking it would do until I found something else, but six weeks later, I was hooked. It turns out my careful observation skills are totally useful. And my dog is in seventh heaven. Apparently Pepe has always dreamed of being a PI.

"No can do, doll," Jimmy G said. "Jimmy G is a little low on the moola."

"What happened to all the money you made on our last case?" I asked. I had been able to catch up on my mortgage payments and had made an appointment with a financial planner to determine how to invest the rest.

Jimmy G shrugged. "Owed some money to the wrong kind of guys. If Jimmy G hadn't paid up, he woulda been sleeping with the fishes."

"I told you, Geri," said Pepe. "We should start our own agency."

"Hush," I told him. "I need to get trained by a licensed PI."

"Speaking of that," said Jimmy G, "I just got a notice about renewing the agency license, too." He began tossing the papers on his desk around. "It's around here somewhere."

"You need to take care of these bills," I said.

"That's why I have a gal Friday," he said.

"How many times do I have to tell you: I am not a girl Friday."

"Administrative assistant?" asked Jimmy G with pathos in his voice.

I have to admit the politically correct term sounded ridiculous when he said it.

"Not that either. I am a private investigator in training," I said. "And we have to clear up these bills so we can keep the agency going." Which reminded me about the framed clipping I had left out in the hall. I went to get it and propped it up on one of the little wooden chairs across from Jimmy G's desk that were there for prospective clients. "Especially since the agency is in the news."

"Speaking of which, that's how Jimmy G got his new case," said Jimmy G.

"The one for me and Geri?" Pepe asked.

"The one for me and Pepe?" I asked.

"Yes, that one. The client read about our last case in the newspaper and called up Jimmy G."

"So who's the client?"

"A man named Mark Darling. His wife has joined a cult and she won't respond to his phone calls or messages. He wants us to get her out."

"Why us?" I asked.

"Because it has to do with a dog," said Jimmy G, beaming.

"Really?" Pepe's ears pricked up at that.

It's true we had solved our last case, which had to do with a dog, but again, it wasn't really on purpose. It was more like we created enough havoc so that we got the results we wanted by accident.

"I hope it involves a bitch," said Pepe.

I was about to chide him when I realized he meant a female dog.

"With a strong aroma and luscious fur," said Pepe.

"I thought Siren Song was the one for you," I told him. Siren Song was an attractive golden Pomeranian. Unfortunately, she was now in Hollywood with her owner, and Pepe's heart was aching.

"*Sí*, Siren Song is the first in my heart," said Pepe. "But a dog's heart is big."

"Siren Song?" Jimmy G asked. "No, the dog's name is Dogawanda. Have you heard of him?"

"Sure," I said.

"I have not," said Pepe.

"He's an ancient dog who speaks through a channeler, a woman by the name of Crystal Star. He has quite a following," I told Pepe.

"Crazy folks!" said Jimmy G, shaking his head.

"Not so loco," said Pepe. "I think all humans could learn much by listening to dogs. I would like to have a following myself."

"So what do you want me to do?" I asked Jimmy G.

"First you have to meet with this Mark Darling.

But the idea is for you to go undercover in the group. Try to make contact with the woman. Deliver her husband's message. Should be simple." Jimmy G rolled his eyes. "Unless you fall for their line of BS."

"Don't worry, boss," I said. "I'm too smart to fall under the spell of a dog."

"Ha!" said Pepe. "That is sarcasm!"

Chapter 2

Mark and Tammy Darling lived in a perfect little Craftsman bungalow in the Ravenna neighborhood of Seattle, a charming older neighborhood full of small homes set back on leafy streets. It was the sort of home I dreamed of owning, and maybe I could afford with all the money I had made on our last case. Pepe insisted that half of the money was his and we were still negotiating about how to spend it. He suggested getting a fancy new car or, at least, a year's supply of beef jerky and bacon.

The front yard looked like an English garden, with its profusion of old-fashioned flowers: hollyhocks and ruffled irises, speckled foxgloves, and bright blue delphiniums. Mirrored ornaments set here and there sparkled in the sun and a glass globe drifted in the waters of the birdbath, an iridescent bubble. Along the fence on the property line, fruit trees had been espaliered. The finishing touch: a cute little red Smart car in the driveway.

A winding brick path led us through the flowers to the front door. The house had a roomy front porch with fat pillars and wide stone steps. The porch was furnished with a swing, draped with a colorful serape. A wind chime hanging from the porch roof tinkled faintly. Pressing the doorbell triggered a sonorous chime and the appearance of a distressed man.

"Come in! Come in!" he said. "Oh, I'm so glad you agreed to help me."

Mark Darling had worried brown eyes behind wire-rimmed glasses and brown hair that stuck up in odd tufts all over his head. I couldn't quite tell if this was due to his running his hands through his hair or if it was an artful effect achieved with hair product. It gave him a youthful appearance, though I judged him to be in his early forties, about ten years older than me.

A little dirty white dog that might have been a mix of poodle and Yorkshire terrier came bustling up as soon as we crossed the threshold. It didn't look like anyone had groomed her for a long time. In her anxious state and unkempt hair, she resembled her owner.

"That's Fuzzy," said Mark, ushering us inside.

Fuzzy and Pepe began sniffing butts and doing that weird jumpy dance dogs do when they're getting to know each other.

"Can I get you anything to drink?" Mark asked, hurrying us through the hallway, past a spacious living room, and into the kitchen, obviously recently redone. The kitchen counters were poured concrete colored a golden hue, and the backsplash was made of translucent leaf-green tiles. Open shelves displayed a collection of orange, yellow, and green Fiesta ware plates and bowls that made me envious. "Coffee? Tea? Lemonade? Water?"

"Gracias," said Pepe, trotting over to Fuzzy's bowl and slurping down the water. He finished up with a mighty sneeze. For some reason, Pepe always inhales some water when he's drinking. Fuzzy sat nearby looking forlorn as Pepe turned his attention to Fuzzy's stainless-steel food bowl.

"Ugh!" said Pepe, turning away after a few mouthfuls. "Bargain brand." He shuddered and shook himself off as he does when something upsets him.

I asked for tea and Mark turned on a stainless-steel electric kettle that was sitting on the counter. The kitchen was immaculate. There were no dirty dishes in the sink. No stains on the stove. It didn't look anything like my house.

"Do you have a cleaning service?" I asked.

Mark seemed startled. "Oh, you mean because the house is so clean?" He looked around. "I guess I got a little carried away. Cleaning is what I do when I'm anxious. It sucks to feel helpless—I just have to keep busy!"

When the water was hot, he poured it into a clear

glass carafe and invited me to join him at the breakfast nook on one end of the kitchen. The windows looked out on a backyard that was even more precious than the front yard. Raised beds full of luxuriant vegetables. A huge state-of-the-art stainless-steel grill on a cobbled patio. Even a bread oven set among herbs.

The sky had been getting increasingly darker. As we watched, the rain began to fall, dripping from the edge of the eaves, spattering against the windows. It was June in Seattle, but we sometimes called this month Juneuary because the weather is not that much different from January. Pepe jumped up onto the bench beside me while Fuzzy lay down on the floor at Mark's feet, putting her head on her paws with a deep sigh.

"Poor Fuzzy," said Mark, taking a sip of his tea. "She's just been moping. I can't believe that Tammy would abandon her."

I found it odd that he wasn't thinking of himself, but maybe he was the kind of guy who always thought of other people first.

"Is Fuzzy particularly attached to Tammy?"

"Yes, Tammy always wanted a dog, but we couldn't have one when we lived in an apartment. So as soon as we bought the house, she went right out to the shelter and came home with that mutt." He took a sip of his tea. "I can't believe she could just walk away from her. And all this." He waved his hand at the yard. It certainly looked like a little bit of paradise.

"How long have you been married?"

"Our anniversary is June twenty-fifth. Next week. Seven years of married bliss." He took a sip of his tea and looked out the rain-smeared window at the garden.

"Do not speak, Geri," said Pepe. "That is good interviewing technique."

Actually, I wasn't going to speak anyway, since I had just helped myself to one of the giant sugar cookies Mark had set out and my mouth was full. The cookies looked and tasted like they were homemade. Was Mark baking as well as cleaning to compensate for his loss?

"I know what you're thinking. That's what the police said. The seven-year itch. She got tired of being married and ran off. But, believe me, there was nothing wrong with our marriage. I mean, we had our share of problems, but we were working on them."

"Ask about the problems," Pepe suggested.

"If you don't mind my asking, what were the problems?"

"Well, of course, that's why you're here," Mark said. He leaned forward. "We wanted children, but we couldn't get pregnant. No matter what we tried and, believe me, we tried everything. Then finally, just when we gave up, Tammy got pregnant. She was so excited."

He took his glasses off and rubbed at his eyes. "She had a miscarriage in the fifth month. It was terrible. She couldn't get over it. That's when those people got a hold of her."

"The Dogawandans?" I asked.

"Yes, she attended a seminar and they filled her head with nonsense. Said it was all meant to be. The baby was not gone but living in a different dimension. And she could be there, too, if she divested herself of all her attachments. She went away for a weeklong retreat at their compound, which is somewhere near Cle Elum, and she never came back."

"How long ago was that?" I asked.

Mark sighed. "Almost a month ago."

"And the police weren't concerned?" I found that hard to believe.

"No. Not after I showed them the note."

"What note?"

He set down his cup, reached into the back pocket of his jeans, and pulled out a worn wallet. He opened it and pried out a piece of much-folded paper. He handed it to me without comment and watched as I unfolded it, carefully, because it had been folded and unfolded so many times it was about to fall apart. The message was written on pale green, lined paper, the kind you find in steno notebooks, like the one I carry for my case notes.

"Read it out loud, Geri!" ordered Pepe.

So I did. It read:

I'm not coming home.
Don't try to make me.
This is the last time you will hear from me.
I am dead to you from this point forward.

Chapter 3

"Not good," grumbled Pepe.

"Pretty ominous!" I agreed, folding it back up and handing it to Mark. "It almost sounds like a suicide note."

He nodded. "Yes, if it weren't for the money, I might think that, too."

"What money?"

"A few days after I got this note in the mail, Tammy withdrew twenty-five thousand dollars from our bank account. I'm positive she gave it to the Dogawandans."

"Geri! That is *mucho dinero*," said Pepe. "And it is all going to a dog!"

"Not to a dog," I said. "To Crystal Star."

"Ridiculous, right?" snapped Mark. "All of our retirement money. She just wiped out our account. I'm investigating whether I can get any of that back. Of course, I immediately cashed out our other accounts and put all the money in my name. I'm not going to let that fraud get her hands on it."

Fraud was a strong word but maybe true—there had been many articles written over the years accusing Crystal Star of being a fraud. No one could believe that she was really channeling an ancient spirit presently housed in the body of an elegant Weimaraner. But I knew better than most people that strange things could happen. As if to illustrate my point, Pepe spoke up again.

"Geri, we must go to meet this woman who can talk to dogs. Once she listens to me, she will throw off this Dogawanda character and make herself an acolyte of Pepe *el Magnifico!*"

We borrowed a photo of Tammy, a vivacious redhead with a wide, freckled face and an infectious grin. I promised to call Mark as soon as we had any information.

I drove straight home to Eastlake. My condo is in an old brick building that was built around the turn of the century and converted to condos in the 1980s. The building has eight units built around a central courtyard. Each has its own front porch, back door, tiny laundry room, small kitchen, small dining room, small bedroom, small bathroom, and a small living room with a bay window. Mine is on the corner and has what they call a pocket view: I can just see a sliver of Lake Union, the urban lake just north of downtown Seattle. I've always loved my home both for its retro charm and its coziness, but it looked cramped after the luscious spaciousness of the Darling home.

I went into the kitchen and scooped out a generous portion of Pepe's favorite wet dog food and plopped it into his bowl. Then while he was chowing down, I went through my cupboards, gathering all the ingredients I needed for the evening meal.

I was making dinner for my boyfriend, Felix, and his brother, who was flying up from L.A. It was going to be a little tricky since Felix and his brother are both carnivores while I'm a vegetarian, so I planned to make a pasta dish.

I had already been to the specialty butcher at Melrose Market and purchased some slices of ham that I planned to dice and add to the portions I served to my guests. I wasn't going to have any even though I had been assured the ham came from a happy free-range pig that had been slaughtered humanely. I was a vegetarian before I adopted Pepe, but once my dog started talking to me, I became even more committed. Not that Pepe understood this. He is most decidedly not a vegetarian and we frequently argue about this.

Albert the Cat came in to rub against my legs, and as soon as he entered the kitchen, Pepe left. They had reached a sort of truce, after some initial dust-ups, where they had agreed not to be in the same space at the same time. Pepe had claimed the living room while Albert the Cat ruled the bedroom, but they had to share the kitchen.

Pepe begged me to turn on my laptop. "I will do research on this Dogawanda character," he said. It was set up on the coffee table in the living room where Pepe could see the screen and use his tiny paws on the touch pad.

So I let him entertain himself while I made sure I had everything I needed for dinner. I checked the items off one by one and was just congratulating myself for being so organized when Pepe called out.

"Come quick, Geri!" he said. "I have found something."

"What is it?" I asked, hurrying into the living room.

"Sit down and see for yourself."

Pepe is pretty skilled at working the computer. He even has a Facebook page and more friends than me. He pushed a button with his paw and an image of a beautiful, fortyish woman appeared on the screen. She had long, frosted blond hair and was dressed in multiple layers of flowing turquoise silk. Her arms were lined with turquoise bracelets and her fingers thick with silver and turquoise rings. Her head was raised skyward, her mouth was open, and the expression on her face was one of sublime ecstasy. On either side of her stood two huge statues of wolves, their heads also raised high, as if they were howling at the moon.

The caption below the photo read:

**DOGAWANDA OFFERS TRUE PATH
TO ENLIGHTENMENT**

I read the story out loud: "'Rock guitarist Fox Black arrived Saturday at the Dogawanda Ranch just a few miles outside of Cle Elum for some one-on-one time with the famous guru, Dogawanda, and his human translator, Crystal Star. Black's manager says his client is "burned out on fame" and is seeking a more meaningful approach to life. The famous lead guitarist is only the latest in a long string of celebrities who have sought counsel from Dogawanda.'"

"Perhaps we are in the wrong business, Geri," said Pepe. "Maybe you should channel me and we, too, could rake in the *dinero*."

"Pepe," I said. "If I could get people to believe that you were a talking dog, we *would* make a fortune."

"You think?" he asked.

"Yes, I do," I said. I followed a link on Crystal Star's page to the Dogawanda Center for Enlightenment. This page showed a blurry photo of a beautiful gray dog who appeared to be floating on a cloud.

"So what does this Dogawanda have to say?" Pepe asked.

"I don't know," I said. "He's not speaking to me the way you do. But apparently somebody has transcribed his sayings." I clicked on a sidebar that read THE WISDOM OF DOGAWANDA, VOLUME I.

"Read it to me, Geri," said Pepe.

So I did: "'In the Before Time, Dogawanda cast off his slavery to all things and became a warrior for Truth. Needing not gold or silver, he traveled the continents spreading enlightenment and tranquility. *Having nothing, you have everything, and everything is the Here and Now,* became his mantra. This is the Word of the Dog.'"

"I like the last part about the dog," said Pepe.

I clicked on another one of the tabs at the top of the screen. This one was labeled EVENTS.

"Oh, this looks good," I said. "Crystal Star is giving an introductory weekend at the Center and it starts tomorrow. It looks like I can still register. Then we'll be able to find Tammy Darling. All we have to do is pretend to be interested in Dogawanda."

"I am interested in Dogawanda," said Pepe. "If Crystal Star knows how to find people who will listen to dogs, I want to meet her!"

Chapter 4

I called the number on the screen, and it was answered right away.

"Oh, I'm so sorry," said the woman on the line, who introduced herself as Lily. "We're completely full for that weekend. It's been sold out for several months." She offered to put my name on the waiting list and asked me for a lot of information, including my credit card number, my birth date, and my address.

"Just in case we have a last-minute cancellation," she said.

I didn't like that, and I wondered how Pepe and I were going to make contact with Tammy Darling if we couldn't get to the Center.

Just then the doorbell rang. It was Felix. I had asked him to help me train Pepe. I hoped it would give us some time together before his brother arrived. We had been dating for over a month, but it was still unclear where the relationship was heading.

"Ready for the training session?" Felix asked after handing me a bouquet of fragrant sweet peas. He looked great as usual, in a pair of chinos and a crisp white T-shirt that set off the caramel color of his skin.

"We will see who trains who!" said Pepe.

"I'm ready," I said, whisking the flowers away and putting them in a vase. "But I'm not sure about Pepe."

Felix turned to Pepe and asked, "Are you ready for some training, my little amigo?"

"Not before I get a treat, hombre," Pepe told him.

As if he understood my dog, Felix pulled a baggie out of the pocket of his scuffed black leather jacket. It contained some crumbled bacon bits. He gave one to Pepe, who quickly devoured it.

"That should soften him up," Felix told me. "There's nothing like a positive reward when working with a dog. He will soon figure out that there's more to come when he learns to obey."

Finished with the last morsel, Pepe said, "Obey this, mister!" and ran to the door, scratching on it to go out.

"Look at that," Felix said with a grin. "He's ready to go."

"Good human!" Pepe praised Felix as he headed to the door. "You came right to me just as I wanted. I think you may do well. Now open the door."

I got Pepe's leash and harness from the hook on

the back of the door, but before I could get them on him, Felix opened the door and Pepe dashed outside.

He got halfway down the block before I managed to grab him and wrestle him into his harness and leash.

"Notice how he walks so far ahead of you," Felix said as we proceeded downhill. The rain had let up, although clouds still covered the sky. Pepe was a few yards ahead of us, at the very end of the retractable leash.

I nodded. This was typical. Pepe always surged ahead of me on our daily rambles. Lately he had taken to impulsively dashing across the street in search of ever more tantalizing aromas, which is what worried me and made me ask for Felix's help.

Felix was an animal trainer. He grew up in L.A. in a show business family and went to school to learn how to work with wild animals on TV and movie sets. When he moved to Seattle (in search of a quieter life, he said, but he had never told me exactly what he meant by that), he went into a more domestic line of business: as a dog trainer, which he said usually involved training the human more than the dog.

"That means Pepe considers himself the alpha," said Felix. "He's scoping out the scene for danger before you enter the picture."

"Do not worry, Geri," said Pepe, whose sensitive long ears had picked up our conversation. "I will protect you." We turned right when the road hit the lake and walked along a street lined with blackberry brambles on one side and parking lots for the houseboat residents on the other.

"How thoughtful," I murmured.

"Not really," said Felix, with a little frown. "*You* need to be the alpha. He should feel certain that you will protect him from harm, not the other way around. It's our job to provide safety for our dogs."

We were heading for a small pocket park on the edge of the lake. Just then, a cyclist buzzed down the hill and zipped into the parking lot, almost crashing into the leash and possibly causing a fatal accident. I had to race ahead to catch up with Pepe, scooping him up and out of the way just in the nick of time. I was trembling when Felix caught up with me.

"That was a close call," Felix said, gathering me into his arms.

He held me until I stopped trembling, and he never once said *I told you so*, which is one of many things I love about Felix. I also love his kindness and his patience, with both people and animals. And it doesn't hurt that he's so handsome, with his brown skin, his high cheekbones, and his dark eyes. I snuggled closer, taking in the scent of his cologne: something spicy and earthy.

"Put me down!" said Pepe. "You are turning me into a Chihuahua pancake!" I set him down on the ground, and he ran off to sniff at the base of a tree.

"So let's work on getting him to come when called," said Felix once I had stopped trembling.

"OK," I said.

"Get him to look at you, then call his name," said Felix. "Like this!" He called Pepe's name and snapped his fingers.

Pepe gave him a glance. I could see the disdain in his expression—maybe it was the drooping ears. His ears are very expressive. Then he walked off in another direction.

"Pepe!" I said. "*Ven aqui.*" Sometimes he responds better to Spanish than to English. But not this time. He didn't even look up but kept his little nose glued to the ground, as if he was intent on some important discovery.

"Just wait for him," said Felix. "He will eventually want to know what you're doing."

"I know what she is doing," said Pepe. "She is listening to bad advice from someone who believes he is the boss of me."

"So who do you think is the boss?" I asked Pepe.

"You are!" said Felix. "You just have to be patient."

"I am!" said Pepe. "Do I not understand the wisdom of the Here and Now?"

"Oh, don't give me that Dogawandan jargon," I said to him.

"Really," said Felix. "Those people? I don't think they have the corner on patience."

"Oh, I wasn't talking to you," I said. "Pepe and I are supposed to go to a seminar taught by a dog. We've been researching it, and now he's rather full of himself."

"He's always full of himself," said Felix.

That got Pepe's attention. He gave a little growl.

Felix laughed. "I don't mean that as an insult. These little dogs always act much bigger than they are. They have to."

"I am a little dog with a big heart and an even bigger spirit," Pepe announced. "Dogs are only limited by their acceptance of limitations."

Just then my cell phone rang. It was Lily from the Dogawanda Center calling to say there had been a last-minute cancellation. Was I still interested in registering for the weekend?

"Of course!" I said.

"Great! I'll e-mail you a map and a list of what you need to bring," she said. She hung up before I could ask if it was OK to bring a dog. I assumed so, since the whole thing revolved around a dog.

"Since when have you been a devotee of Doga-wanda?" Felix asked as we headed back to my condo. We had given up on training Pepe. Felix had tried all the techniques he knew, but Pepe seemed to be impervious to all of them. He made it clear that he was going to do the opposite of what-ever Felix wanted him to do, bacon or no bacon.

"I'm not a Dogawandan," I told Felix. "It's just that Pepe and I have to deliver a message to a woman who's up at their ranch."

"Just be careful," said Felix as we headed up the stairs and into my condo. "I know someone who got involved in one of these cults in L.A. It's much easier to get in than it is to get out."

"I don't know why everyone's so worried about

me," I said, a little more sharply than I intended. I closed the front door and hung up Pepe's leash and harness on the hook on the back of the door. "It's not like I'm that gullible."

"No, it's just that you always see the best in everyone," said Felix, pressing me up against the wall and delivering one of his great kisses. Combined with his body pressed against mine, it was doing amazing things to me.

"Geri, I would not do that if I were you," said Pepe.

"What? Leave me alone!" I managed to murmur.

Felix stepped back, a hurt look on his face.

"I wasn't talking to you," I said, drawing him back toward me. "I was talking to Pepe. He was complaining about something."

"You are so attentive to his needs," said Felix. "What about mine?" And he moved his body against me in ways that made it clear what his needs were. In fact, it made it clear what I needed. It had been way too long since I had gotten any action. Felix and I were always being interrupted just as we were about to tumble into bed.

"I am trying to tell you, Geri. Somebody is on the front porch," Pepe said.

Chapter 5

He was right. When I opened the door, there was a man on my front porch, holding a six-pack of beer. I recognized him instantly as Felix's brother—they have the same wide grin. He was dressed in worn jeans and a T-shirt but seemed fine despite the misty rain. But his female companion wasn't prepared for the Seattle weather. She wore a flimsy dress and was shivering, her arms wrapped around her body.

"Whoa! You startled me!" said the man. "I haven't even rung the doorbell yet. You must have ESP."

"No," I said. "I have a dog."

"Geri, this is my brother, Tavo," said Felix, clapping him on the back.

"Short for Gustavo," said Tavo. "I was named after our grandfather. But please never call me that." He smiled and offered me his hand. "It's good to meet you, Geri."

"And this is Chloe," said Felix. She had long

blond hair, big brown eyes, a pretty upturned nose, and a pretty downturned mouth.

"Chloe's the star of the film we're working on," said Tavo. "You might recognize her. She was the star of *Zombies Gone Wild*."

Not very likely. I do like horror movies, but I hadn't seen one since my divorce. Too scary to watch alone. And Pepe refuses to watch them. He prefers telenovelas and reality TV shows.

"Glad to meet you," I said.

"Tavo!" said Felix. "I thought I was supposed to pick you up." He checked his watch. "Did I get the time wrong?"

"No, I managed to get a seat on an earlier flight. Chloe was on the same plane and so I invited her along," Tavo said. "Since I knew you weren't expecting me so early, I decided to rent a car. Thought I'd save you the trip to the airport."

"I don't see how you can stand to live in a climate like this," Chloe said to me, still shivering. I pulled a towel out of the linen closet and directed her toward the bathroom where she could dry herself off. I also offered her one of my favorite cardigans, which I thought was very nice of me, as it was one of my favorites: a shell-pink number with silver flowers embroidered up and down the placket.

"Is this OK, Geri?" Felix asked, coming into the kitchen, putting his arms around me and whispering in my ear. Tavo was in the dining room opening the beer. I could hear the pop and fizz of the cans as the pressure was released. "Tavo felt sorry for

Chloe since she didn't know anyone in Seattle and invited her along."

"Yeah, sure," I said. "Why don't you go keep them busy while I finish up the dinner preparations? We should be ready to eat in about fifteen minutes."

Felix gave me a kiss on the cheek, then went out into the dining room. I set the water on to boil for the pasta. Normally I might have felt rushed, but since I had everything prepped, dinner would be a snap.

I was just setting another place at the table for Chloe when she came back from the bathroom, still wearing my sweater, I noted. I offered her a glass of wine, but she said she preferred water.

Once the pasta was done, I whipped up some of my homemade dressing: a raspberry vinaigrette. We all gathered at the table, and Tavo and Felix made appreciative noises as they sat down to eat, but Chloe pouted. It turned out she was vegan, so she couldn't eat the pasta because of the cheese, not to mention the ham. I offered to share the small meatless portion I had set aside for myself, but she declined my offer.

"Is that your dog?" she asked. Pepe was circling her ankles as if he thought they might be good to eat.

"Yes, that is Pepe," I said, thinking she would reach down and pet him, which is what most people do when they see Pepe.

Instead she shuddered. "Please get him away

from me. I don't like dogs. I got bit once when I was a kid."

"Go watch TV," I told Pepe.

"Your dog watches TV?" Tavo asked as I sat down at the table.

"He loves telenovellas," I said, pouring my home-made dressing over my salad. "Of all the Spanish soap operas, *Paraiso Perdido* is his favorite."

"Can you believe what Ramon did last week?" Tavo asked.

"What did he do?" I asked.

"He turned his own brother over to the *federales*," Tavo said, twirling some of the pasta noodles around his fork.

"*Sí*, his brother is a big drug lord, and he will have his men after Ramon now for sure," said Pepe. He was licking his lips, no doubt waiting for some ham to come his way.

"Pepe, go watch the next episode," I said. "And you can tell us what happens."

"I can tell you right now what will happen," said Pepe. "Ramon better go into hiding. Preferably at the home of Conchita." But he went trotting off into the living room.

"He obeys you now," said Felix.

"Yes," I said with a sigh. "He's very good at doing what he wants."

"He can turn on the TV?" Tavo asked.

"He can operate the remote," I said. "He's highly motivated when it comes to entertainment." I heard the click of the TV coming on in the living room.

"Amazing!" Tavo said. "Does my brother get any credit?"

"No," said Felix, helping himself to another serving of the pasta. "Geri is the only one who can train this Chihuahua. I'll have to settle for working with bigger dogs."

Unfortunately, I had also dressed the salad with crumbled feta, along with roasted walnuts and chopped fennel root. Chloe was picking her way through the salad, removing the crumbly white chunks of feta and making a little mountain of them on her plate.

"So tell me about your movie," I said.

"It's an independent project. Low-budget horror," Tavo said. "I've worked with the director before. He's pretty easygoing. Should be fun. Plus I knew I could spend some time with Felix since we're filming up here in Seattle. Then it turned out they needed a trainer for the wolves."

I guess I looked puzzled.

"It's a werewolf movie," Tavo said.

"Werewolves are the new vampires," said Chloe.

"So you'll be working with real wolves?" I turned to Felix. This was the first time he had worked with wild animals since I had known him.

Felix shrugged. "Not wolves, wolf-hybrids. But some are probably seventy-five percent wolf. Which means they're almost as unpredictable as real wolves."

"Isn't that dangerous?"

"Not if I can help it," he said. "It's my job to make sure they look menacing but behave like pussycats."

"You wouldn't say that," I said, "if you knew my cat, Albert."

"Felix is good," Tavo said. "Did you know he worked with the wolves in the *True Blood* series?"

Felix shook his head, his eyes warning his brother not to pursue that line of thought. It gave me the impression that it hadn't been a good experience for him.

"No, I didn't," I said. I threw Felix a look that meant *Why have you never told me about this?*

"Just as long as you keep them away from me," said Chloe. She set down her fork. Her plate was empty except for the little mound of discarded cheese bits. "Can we go, Tavo? I'm really tired."

"I want to hang out with my little bro," Tavo said. "Why don't you take the car to the hotel? Felix can give me a ride later."

Chloe didn't like that idea, it was obvious, but she was finally persuaded and left, in my favorite sweater, without even saying good-bye or thank you. I guess stars can be pretty self-centered, especially when they are beautiful. Of course, I didn't really like the idea either. I was hoping for some one-on-one time with Felix.

We adjourned to the living room, the men with the last two beers and me with another glass of wine. Pepe was curled up on a pillow on the sofa when we walked in.

"How was *Paraiso Perdido*?" I asked him.

"Tell Senor Tavo he was right," said Pepe. "Ramon is now hiding in the closet at Conchita's casa."

"He says you were right," I told Tavo. "About Ramon, that is."

"I often am," said Tavo. "Privilege of being the older brother."

Felix gave him a playful punch in the arm. Apparently this was part of their bonding ritual.

"What about you?" Tavo asked. "Do you have siblings?"

"I'm the middle one of three sisters," I said.

"And is your older sister always right?" asked Felix.

"Cheryl certainly thinks so," I said.

"No. I am the one who is always right," said Pepe.

"And what about your younger sister?" Tavo asked. "Does she get her way by being cute and charming like Felix here?"

I tried to smile. "It's hard to say."

Felix jumped in, trying to save me from an awkward conversation.

"Geri hasn't seen her younger sister in a while," he said. It was a topic we had discussed briefly on our first date. But we had never talked about it since. It's not something I like to talk about.

Tavo didn't get the hint. "Really?" He sounded puzzled. "Does she live overseas?" Obviously he didn't understand a family where the siblings weren't close.

"No," I said. I really didn't need to say more

than that, but the words came tumbling out. "She disappeared years ago. Naturally Cheryl and I fear the worst. That she's dead. But then the alternative is just as bad. If she is alive, how could she be so cruel as to not let us know?"

The mood had become very solemn.

"But I am going to find her for Geri!" Pepe announced.

"Maybe that's why you became a PI," said Tavo. "So you could find her."

"That's exactly what I told her!" Felix said. The two brothers smiled at each other, happy to share a common thought.

I tried to smile, too, but it was hard. I had been searching for Terry on and off with little success. I tried to lighten the mood. "So if that's why I became a PI, why did you become a wild animal trainer?" I asked Felix.

"Ha! That's easy!" said Tavo. "Living in our house growing up was like living in a three-ring circus."

Chapter 6

We had to leave early the next morning to make it up to the Dogawanda ranch, so maybe it was a good thing Felix didn't stay over. I was nervous as I drove out of Seattle, since I had never gone undercover before, but Pepe was in fine form. He stood at the passenger window, his forepaws on the armrest, drinking in the forest and mountain views as we drove higher and higher over Snoqualmie Pass east of Seattle.

Pepe was napping by the time we got to the summit of the pass. Still napping while we drove along the length of Keechelus Lake. And still napping when I took the exit for Fern Lake. According to the map, the Dogawanda Center was up in the mountains north of that town.

Instead of turning right into the town, I took a left, on a feeder road that led up into the mountains. There were no other cars in sight. I rolled my window down, and even at this high elevation, a balmy breeze was blowing. The scent of evergreens filled the car. Two chipmunks chased each other across the road.

The road narrowed and the trees grew taller. The light dimmed. It seemed like I'd been driving forever, and I began to worry that I had missed a turnoff. Then I saw a wooden sign welcoming me to the Dogawanda Center for Enlightenment.

I turned off onto a long gravel covered driveway that ended in a dirt parking lot full of cars, most of them SUVs and a few luxury sedans. There was one car that stood out among the rest: a shiny, bright red sports car that looked like it was moving a hundred miles an hour even when standing still.

"That is Fox Black's famous Lamborghini Countach," said Pepe.

"Are you sure?" I asked my dog.

"Of course," he said. "I once saw it on the Spanish MTV channel. They showed him driving all over L.A. with a bunch of beautiful women in that car."

"I used to listen to his band all the time when I was in high school," I said.

"Well, maybe we will meet him," said Pepe. "Right now, let us park the car. I want to get out and mark my new territory."

I tucked my beaten-up green Toyota into the far corner of the lot, and Pepe and I hiked across the parking lot toward the front gate. Pepe sniffed his way along the tires, muttering to himself, and occasionally stopped to leave his mark.

I wondered if it was a problem that I had brought my dog. Maybe there was room for only one dog at the ranch.

The front gate was set into a chain-link fence, topped with curled razor wire, which stretched away on either side into the woods. The actual gate, a wooden door crisscrossed with iron bands and swinging on metal hinges, was framed by heavy side beams and a sturdy roof.

Two acolytes stood in front of the door: a man and a woman both dressed in green-dyed cotton clothing: flowing pants and a simple tunic top. The woman who introduced herself as Sequoia checked off my name on a list and asked for Pepe's name, too. The man, who said his name was Sky, asked to see my driver's license and checked it against my appearance.

"Does everyone take a new name?" I asked.

"Once you have graduated to the beta pack, Dogawanda gives you a new name," the man said, looking me over.

I wondered if he would approve of the outfit I had chosen. It had been difficult to know what to wear to a spiritual retreat, and I had finally decided on a vintage embroidered Mexican blouse over jeans.

Pepe didn't approve and had told me so. Since he once lived in Beverly Hills, he has high standards, but the guard didn't seem to object to my outfit. He nodded as he handed my license back to me.

"Why all the security?" I asked.

The man frowned. "Sometimes a journalist tries to sneak in undercover. We want to ensure privacy for all of our guests."

"So it's not just because Fox Black is here?" I asked.

He shook his head. "These are our normal precautions."

Sequoia lit a sage stick and began wafting it around my head and whisking the smoke in my direction with a big feather.

"What is she doing to you, Geri?" Pepe asked. "Trying to make you smell more like them?"

It was almost as if she could hear him. "This is a purification process," she said. "The smoke of white sage grown on the property. It helps to clear away any negative energy you may be bringing with you." She circled around me.

"I think my dog needs some attitude adjustment," I said.

"Oh no," she assured me. "Dogs already live in the moment and do not hold on to negativity."

"So there, Geri!" said Pepe, dashing through the door as Sequoia opened it.

"You would be surprised," I said, running after Pepe.

We went up a dirt path that wound through a grove of tall evergreens, until it came out on a rise, overlooking a cleared area that contained several buildings. There was a magnificent old lodge, made out of huge half-timbered logs, at the far side of the clearing. In the meadow at the right was a huge teepee-like structure. According to the map, it was a yurt. Other buildings filled the space between: a long low building, covered with brush and sod (the map said it was the Longhouse), a long low building that looked like it belonged in Southern California (the map said it was the Bunkhouse), and a huge old-fashioned whitewashed barn (the map said it was the Barn). The map also showed other features: a fire pit in front of the lodge, a garden behind the yurt, and a hot springs accessed by a path that wound through the woods.

I was supposed to register in the lobby of the lodge, so we headed there. Wide, shallow steps led up to a spacious front porch lined with rustic chairs fashioned out of twigs and wicker. Inside the lodge, huge beams punctuated a voluminous space overhead. A river-rock fireplace dominated one wall. The air smelled like cedar.

The woman who sat behind the table directly in front of the front doors introduced herself as Artichoke. She was also dressed in leaf-green, hand-dyed cotton: a long skirt and a camisole top. Her bare skin was brown from the sun, and she wore her dark hair in a braid twisted on top of her head.

"Thank Dog you are here!" she said. "You are the last to arrive. Now we can begin." She checked off our names on her list, then handed me a dark-green paper portfolio containing an agenda, a map, and a name tag that I was to wear during the weekend.

"No name tag for my dog?" I said jokingly as I slipped the elastic over my neck and straightened the plastic holder in which the card bearing my name was displayed.

She stood up and stared over the edge of the table at Pepe. "You were not supposed to bring a dog with you!"

"But I thought he would benefit from the wisdom of the Dog," I said, trying to make a joke.

"Dogawanda's wisdom is for us humans. Dogs already live in the timeless Now," she said.

"That is so true!" said Pepe.

"What's next?" I asked.

"Go to your room and familiarize yourself with the contents of the packet," she told me. "The first workshop will begin in about fifteen minutes. The schedule for the weekend is in the folder I just gave you."

We were assigned a room in the Bunkhouse, the building that looked like a California mission. The outside walls were whitewashed stucco and the roof was covered with red tiles. Inside the room was monastic but pleasant. There was a single bed, covered with a dark wool blanket, a tiny bathroom with just a toilet and a sink, and a window that looked out over the woods. It smelled like incense, but the incense was covering up something older and less pleasant—perhaps mildew.

We each had our own way of settling in. Pepe sniffed around the edges of the room, then disappeared under the bed. I began unpacking, putting my folded clothes in the wooden chest of drawers, hanging up my sweaters and coat on the hooks by the door. Then a bell rang, the solemn sound reverberating through the grounds. A quick check of the schedule indicated that the introductory lecture was about to begin.

The map directed us to go to the Longhouse. At the front door, a fair-haired young man named Smoke inspected my name badge before admitting us.

The ceiling was low and the air smelled like dust and cedar. The participants sat on two long rows of benches against the walls, all looking toward what appeared to be a stage that jutted out in a V at one end. Women far outnumbered the men, and most of the men seemed to have come with a partner. I looked around for Tammy but didn't see her; I didn't really expect to see her at an introductory session, unless she was an assistant. Two of the green-clad acolytes were busy setting up items on the stage, a chair plumped with orange silk pillows, and a wooden box, draped with a gold damask cloth.

They sat down, one to the left and one to the right of the stage, and we all waited in silence for many minutes. Suddenly a curtain to the side was parted and Crystal Star appeared, with a gorgeous Weimaraner at her side. She wore a lime-green caftan that fell to the ground, and her blond bouffant hair was piled high on her head. She swept up to the prow of the stage and looked over us. The Weimaraner moved slowly, his legs stiff. His muzzle was almost completely white. He needed a little help from one of the acolytes to get up to the gold-draped platform, where he lay down, resting his head on his paws and looking over us. With his piercing golden-brown eyes, one could easily believe he was a superior being.

"Hello. I am Crystal Star. And this is Max." Star waved her hand at the dog. "An ordinary dog before he was chosen by Dogawanda to be his vessel. A succession of dogs, throughout the centuries, has been thus honored by Dogawanda. Because of my proximity to Max, I am able to access Dogawanda and channel his wisdom for all of you."

She looked out over the assembled group, her gaze roving down one row and up the other. She took her time, making contact with each member of the audience. When she reached me, she locked her eyes to mine for the longest time. She had startling, almost golden eyes. They were as piercing as the Weimaraner's were soulful. It seemed an eternity passed as she held my gaze. Finally I had to look down.

The next thing I knew she had stepped off the platform and come down the length of the hall and was standing right in front of me.

"I see you have brought a little brother with you," she told me, her voice loud enough for all to hear.

"Well, yes," I said. "I thought it would be OK. I—"

"Of course it is right and good that you have brought your companion with you," Star said. "Dogawanda welcomes *all* his brothers and sisters. Especially the canine species, as dogs always speak only the truth."

"She has that part right," Pepe told me.

"You see?" Star said loudly to the entire audience. "This Chihuahua is speaking truth right now." She turned her focus to Pepe again. "Let me channel more of your truth, little brother."

"I came here to learn how to do what you do," said Pepe.

"Ah yes!" she exclaimed, addressing the audience once more. "He says he is excited for us to begin! And so we shall!"

Chapter 7

"Wow! She got it almost right!" I said as she swept back to the front of the room. I was a little bit jealous. After all, I thought I was the only one who could hear Pepe speak.

"Merely a good guess," said Pepe. "She is good at reading people, or dogs, as the case may be. I can sense that about her."

Star stood facing the crowd. "Before I channel Dogawanda, there is a distinction you must understand. I am a channel, not a medium. A medium stays in her body providing a conduit for the spirits. A channel leaves her body completely, allowing the spirit to fully occupy her vessel. With that understanding, I am now ready to channel Dogawanda. Listen carefully to his wisdom—too few have this opportunity."

A hush fell over the crowd. She seated herself in the thronelike chair and put out one hand to rest on the head of the aged but magnificent dog, who stayed absolutely still, gazing out at the audience with those golden eyes.

Star's eyes closed. She shuddered, then lifted her head. Her posture had changed. She seemed to have grown larger, to fill the chair. Her eyes were bright and shining. She smiled wide, her teeth showing brightly.

"Here am I, Dogawanda," she said in a voice unlike her own—a voice gruff, abrupt, with a rough cadence. "Since the Before Time."

A few people gasped.

"Dogawanda is pleased," *he* said, addressing all of us.

The hackles on Pepe's back rose. His lip curled a bit.

There were several titters from the audience.

"Healthy is skepticism," said Dogawanda. "The skeptic is alert. However, too much thinking can make one unwise. I had no need of thought when I rode with Hannibal's elephants into battle. The greatest times of peace always follow the greatest times of war. Therefore, the war within one's self is not to be feared or avoided—rather it is to be accepted, for when the battle is won, peace and enlightenment will surely follow."

Dogawanda paused, then thrust out a *paw*, pointing directly at Pepe. "As with you, Chihuahua!" he said. "You have warred a lifetime against your *little* body. Only when your struggle is won and you accept that you are indeed a *big* Chihuahua, will you taste true peace and tranquility."

"I know that," Pepe said. His voice quavered and was very small.

"And you, Ben!" Dogawanda pointed at the squat, bald man seated to our right. "Your wealth will increase but only if you give it away!"

Ben squirmed a little at that.

"And you, Angela!" Dogawanda continued, pointing at a middle-aged woman across from us. "Reconstructing your face will not win back your mate. Instead you should focus on enriching your mind!"

Angela looked amazed.

I cowered in my seat. I did not want Dogawanda to make a comment about me. But he did.

"And you, Geri!" said Dogawanda. "Your divorce brought you good fortune and your good fortune will lead you to enlightenment."

"She spoke the truth, Geri," said Pepe. "I, naturally, am your good fortune."

I gave him a pat on the head.

"Time is a conundrum," Dogawanda continued. "It is both fleeting and enduring. It is said there is no time like the present, but here is the paradox: When you formulate a thought, it is in the past when you finish it. Paradoxically, it is also in the future while you are formulating it. The present exists only in between. Dogs know this. We exist in the present and thus we know a peace and serenity like no others."

That made some sort of sense. Dogs do seem to

have a simple ability to enjoy life that we humans are missing.

"If you wish to learn the Way of the Dog, you must commit to a rigorous course of training. As a soldier learns to obey his commander, without hesitation, so a dog learns to respond to his trainer, without thought."

"That is surely not right," said Pepe.

"The modern world seduces us with many choices," Dogawanda went on. "But living in the here and now is simple. One can experience constant bliss if one is willing to submit to the will of the One who has loved you since the beginning of time and follow the Way of the Dog. You will learn more of this path throughout this weekend."

"I can teach you the Way of the Dog!" Pepe offered.

"I must now return to Max, my canine vessel," Dogawanda continued. "But Crystal Star, my human vessel, will teach you the Seven Commandments of Dogawanda. Learn them well, for they are the keys to eternal peace. Aloha."

Star shuddered, then slumped forward. When she raised her head again, she seemed dazed. Her eyes blinked rapidly. She stood and swayed. One of the assistants stepped forward and gave her an arm.

"Aloha?" said Pepe.

"It means 'until we meet again,'" I told him.

"So sayeth Dogawanda," said Star, holding out her cupped hands. She bowed her head. The audience applauded. "And now for the Seven Commandments of Dogawanda," she said. "It is important

that you memorize these, as they will guide you through the twisting paths toward the one true way that leads to Dogawanda."

She exhorted us to stand and repeat back to her the following commandments:

1. All roads lead to Dogawanda.
2. Obey your alpha.
3. The pack always knows best.
4. One must walk the twisting path with eyes shut and mind open.
5. If you are not the predator, you are the prey.
6. Create your own pack.
7. Reality is every possible outcome.

When she was satisfied we had learned these, we were dismissed with the command, "Dog be with you!" and told to return after dinner.

We ate our meals in the dining hall, which was in a wing on the ground floor of the lodge. Dinner was served as a buffet, with servers standing behind curved glass, and meals presented in silver chafing dishes. To my dismay, the first items offered were fish and steak.

"But I'm a vegetarian," I said to the server who asked me what I wanted.

"But this is an animal who grazed freely on grass and was killed with mercy," she said, her fork poised in midair, holding a dripping slab of meat.

"I don't really care how it lived," I said. "I don't eat cows."

"I do," said Pepe, looking up with glistening eyes at the hunk of cow meat.

"I'll take a small piece for my dog," I said.

"I would like a large piece, *por favor*," said Pepe, but I ignored him.

"How about fish?" the server asked, moving over to the next pan, which was packed with silvery trout. She slid her spatula under one. "Caught in the pure waters of a lake only a few miles from here, just yesterday."

I considered it for a minute, but the staring eyes of the fish seemed to accuse me of having a hand in its death.

"No thank you," I said, passing down the line, where I was offered a selection of vegetables: spinach, chard, baby greens, carrots, and broccoli. I heaped my plate with those, then added a scoop of raw almonds for some protein. I paused at the end of the line and looked around.

"Where's the silverware?" I asked, speaking more to myself than to anyone else.

"We are serving the diet eaten by our ancestors in Paleolithic times," said the woman who was arranging grapes and apples on a tiered display at the end of the line. "We eat with our fingers as our ancestors did." She wore her hair in a long braid, and I could see that it had a red tint. As she turned around to face me, I caught a glimpse of her face. She was, without a doubt, Tammy Darling.

"Tammy?" I said.

Chapter 8

She looked startled. She glanced left and then right to see if anyone was listening. "My name is Leaf."

"Geri, she is frightened," said Pepe. "You must reassure her or she will not speak to you."

"What a pretty name," I said. "I'm hoping that Dogawanda will bless me with a beautiful name like yours."

"Yes, I was lucky," she said. She leaned in closer. "Crystal's top aide is named Artichoke. Can you imagine?"

"They are all named after fruits and vegetables?" Pepe asked me.

"I guess so," I told him.

"They better not try to name me after a plant or vegetable," said Pepe. "Though come to think of it, I would not mind being called Towering Cedar."

"What a cute little dog," said Tammy, gazing down

at Pepe with sad eyes. "He reminds me of my little girl, Fuzzy. I miss her so much."

"Weren't you allowed to bring a dog with you?" I asked.

"Oh no," she said. "We give up everything that ties us to our mundane lives."

I almost dropped my plate. "I would never give up my dog!" I said.

She gave me a sad smile. "I thought the same when I first came here, but when the wisdom of Dogawanda permeates your spirit, you stop missing those things you previously used to fill up the holes in your spirit."

"I do not fill up the holes in your spirit," Pepe said to me.

Tammy was still gazing longingly at Pepe.

"Would you like to join us for dinner?" I asked.

"I must get permission from my alpha," she said.

"Alpha?"

"That's what we call the leader of our pack," she said, and scurried off.

Pepe and I found a place to sit at a round picnic table out on the redwood deck in back of the main lodge. There was a pleasant view of a little lawn sloping down to the edge of the woods. Huge boulders reared up out of the earth and tall firs and pines left a litter of needles underneath them. The sun was shining, but a light breeze kept the temperature comfortable.

I cut up the beef into small bites and set them down on the wood of the deck.

"Geri, do you expect me to eat off the ground?" Pepe asked.

"Like a wild dog," I said. "Think Paleolithic!"

He thought about that for a minute, then attacked the beef, shaking it back and forth in his teeth as if he had just made a fresh kill.

"Nice work!" I said.

Leaf slid onto the bench across from me with a plate of her own, heaped with vegetables and a slice of beef.

"Flicker gave me permission to talk with you," she said. "She hopes that my faith will help light your way along the path of Dogawanda."

"Flicker?" I still couldn't get used to the weird names.

"That's my alpha. She is one of the inner circle, Star's most trusted assistants. I am so lucky to be part of her pack."

"Tell me about your life," I said. "What did you do before?"

"There is no before," she said. "There is only now."

"Oh, I meant, what did you do in the past?"

"There is no past. Only the present," she replied.

Hmmm. This was going to be difficult. "What do you do to make a living?" I asked. To give her an example, I added, "I stage houses." That wasn't totally a lie since that was what I did before working for Jimmy G.

"There is no need to make a living. All is provided for us. We have food and pure water. The sun and the stars and the wind bringing scents to delight our noses. The abuse and dissent of the world dissolve here. Wisdom and harmony abound."

"Sounds like she is quoting something," said Pepe.

"I'm sure it's Dogawanda," I said.

"All is Dogawanda," said Tammy. She closed her eyes and recited, "'The Now is like footprints in the sand. The tide washes in, and the tide washes out.'"

I decided it was time to deliver my message.

"Fuzzy stopped eating since you left. She is pining away for you."

"What?" Tammy's eyes opened wide.

"Fuzzy. She misses you!"

She stood up abruptly. "How do you know about Fuzzy?"

"Your husband, Mark, hired us to find you. He wants you to come home."

She looked at her plate with a furrowed brow, then pushed it away from her. Again she looked to one side and then the other, as if she thought someone would listen in on our conversation. But the nearest diners were a few yards away.

"You don't understand. I can't leave," she whispered.

"You mean they are holding you prisoner?" I asked, aghast.

"No." She glanced around again. "It's just that no one can leave without finishing the levels. Dogawanda says that once you have opened your mind, you cannot go back into the mundane world. The negativity there will overwhelm you. Only if you pass the fourth level can you reenter the world. Like Fox Black."

"Fox Black is a level four?" I asked.

"Geri, focus!" said Pepe. "We are not here to meet an idol from your past but to deliver a message. And I would like some more of that beef, please."

"Can I have some of the beef on your plate?" I asked Tammy. "Pepe is still hungry."

"His name is Pepe?"

"You can call me Towering Cedar," he said, jumping up on the bench.

"Sometimes he goes by Towering Cedar," I said.

"Yes, Fox Black has been through all the levels. He is one of the very few who can go back out into the world. But you see how it affects him. He must come back here after every tour to reassemble the atoms that have been scrambled by his contact with those who still live in the darkness."

"Ha!" said Pepe.

"What did Mark want you to tell me?" Tammy asked.

"He said he missed you," I said. Although come to think of it, he never actually said those words.

"That's odd," she said. "I would think he'd be more concerned about the money."

"Well, yes, he did mention that," I said. "He was upset about the twenty-five grand. He said he had closed all your other joint accounts."

Tammy looked horrified. "Oh no, that's terrible!

I just signed up for level three. I will be in so much trouble!" She jumped up and went dashing off, her braid swishing back and forth. I watched her disappear into the lodge, not realizing that would be the last time I would see her alive.

Pepe had polished off the last of the beef and was licking his lips. "I think I could get used to this Paleolithic diet," he said.

I poked at the greens on my plate. I like salad but I still felt hungry. "I don't think I can take any more of this," I said. "And besides, we have delivered our message. I guess we can leave."

Chapter 9

"First, let us explore our surroundings," said Pepe. "It has been a long time since I have had the pleasure of being in the wilderness. Let us commune with nature. Perhaps I can find a truffle for you."

"A truffle? You mean those very expensive mushrooms that people use to garnish dishes in expensive restaurants?"

"*Sí*, the very thing. Only, Geri, they are not mushrooms. To be correct, they are fungus. I was trained as a truffle dog during my sojourn in the south of France."

"You've got to be kidding," I said.

"Au contraire," he said. Once in a while, he slips in some French. Just enough to make me wonder. "And I have heard there are truffles to be found in the Northwest woods. This is my first opportunity to explore for myself." He dashed off toward an opening in the edge of the woods and I followed.

Very quickly the day grew dim as the trees filtered the daylight.

"What are you doing?" I asked, following along behind him. He kept dashing off the path and pushing his nose through the loose pine needles.

"I'm sniffing for just the right spot," he told me. He moved farther and farther away, slipping under bushes, going where I couldn't follow.

"Pepe!" I called again. "Where are you?"

"Over here," came his voice off to my left.

"I can't see you!" I called out. "Come back!" I wish I had paid more attention when Felix was trying to teach me how to get him to come when he was called.

I hurried down the path, only to stop with a jolt. In front of me was a long narrow pen that stretched back into the woods. It was topped with the same razor wire I had seen at the front gate. There was a little hut at one end. The ground behind the fence had been cleared; it was just raw dirt.

"Pepe!" I called. I really didn't like the look of it. Something in the atmosphere wasn't right. I felt a prickle at the back of my neck.

"What is it, Geri?" said Pepe, hurrying to my side. I have to admit, he is very good at staying close when he thinks I am in trouble.

"Why would anybody build a pen here?" I asked my dog.

"I do not know," said Pepe. "But there is a strong scent here." He lifted his leg and put his own scent on the fence, then started to saunter back toward me.

Bam! In a flash of snarling gray fur and slashing teeth and glowing yellow eyes, two wolves crashed into the chain-link fence, just inches from Pepe. They were long, rangy beasts, with wickedly sharp fangs.

Pepe jumped back, then turned to face them, his little lip lifted and a tiny growl emitting from his throat.

"Let's get out of here, Pepe!" I said, bending down to scoop him up.

"Let me speak to them, Geri," Pepe said. "Are they not my relatives?" He faced the pen and spoke to the wolves.

"I come to you in peace," he said. "I am your cousin from the desert."

The wolves seemed to understand him. They stopped their snarling and, unbelievably, lay down in front of my dog.

"There," said Pepe, his tone very soothing, "that is more polite." He said a few other things in Spanish, and the wolves nodded and whined like little puppies.

"Pepe," I said, still feeling a bit nervous, "how did you do that?"

He turned to me and said proudly, "Elementary, my dear Sullivan. When a Chihuahua and a wolf go *perro a perro*, the best dog always wins." He laughed and added, "*Seriamente*, though, I simply calmed them with my dulcimer voice. They knew I was not a threat, and they certainly knew *you* were no threat."

I didn't know if I should be insulted by that or

not but felt it was high time to get away from there. Those wolves were obviously meant to guard the ranch, and I didn't want to take any chances.

We were heading back to the room when one of the green-clad acolytes approached us. This time it was an older man with a salt-and-pepper beard and gold-rimmed glasses. He introduced himself as Flint.

"The enlightened one requests the honor of your company," he said.

"What?"

"The enlightened one would like to speak to you," he repeated.

"I think he means Dogawanda," Pepe said.

"Do you mean Dogawanda?"

"Yes, he is very interested in your little companion," Flint said, bowing in Pepe's direction. "He wishes to converse with him on matters of great importance for the world. Would you follow me, please?"

I looked at Pepe, unsure of what to do.

"Finally," said Pepe, trotting after the guy, his little tail wagging, "someone who wants to listen to me."

Chapter 10

Flint took us along a curving path that led behind the buildings and toward the yurt that stood in the center of the higher meadow at the far end of the property. It was about thirty feet tall and was constructed of hides draped over multiple wooden poles. From the open door one could see out across a valley of evergreens and up to the snow-capped peaks of the Cascade Range. Behind it was a fenced garden where I could see green-clad acolytes working among a tangle of plants and flowers growing in raised beds.

"You are very lucky," Flint said. "The yurt is reserved for private sessions with Dogawanda. Usually you have to be a level four before you get a chance to meet with him one-on-one."

"What level are you?" I asked. "How long does it take to get to level four?"

"I'm only a level three," he said. "Very few make it to level four."

"What would it take to get to level four?"

He shrugged. "It depends. Dogawanda decides when you are ready."

"So how many people are at level four?" I asked, knowing already that Fox Black was a level four.

"Maybe seven of the people in the inner circle," he said.

"The inner circle?"

"Star's personal assistants. And a couple of celebrities who come here regularly, like Fox Black."

Just as he was saying this, the flap that hung over the door lifted, and Fox Black appeared. He was wearing ripped jeans and a tight T-shirt on his skinny frame. His arms were covered with tattoos. He tossed back his long, dark hair as he emerged to get it out of his eyes and then stopped and stared at me and Pepe.

"So this is the lucky little fellow," he said, looking over Pepe but also checking me out from head to toe and back again. He held out a hand. "Fox Black," he said.

"I . . . I know," I stammered, putting out my hand. "I'm a big fan." Well, that certainly seemed lame. But he didn't seem fazed. Must be used to women falling apart in his presence. This close up to him, it was easy to see the ravages of his lifestyle: the sunken cheekbones, the dark circles under his eyes, the unhealthy pallor of his skin. But he was still so sexy with those dark, piercing eyes and those thick, luscious lips. . . .

Oh my God, he was bringing my hand up to his

mouth. He was nibbling on the back of my hand with those big, sexy lips. I suddenly became light-headed. He smelled like incense and jasmine.

"Geri," said Pepe. "Please exercise some self-control."

Flint had gone ahead into the yurt. With one last long lingering look at Fox Black, I followed Pepe inside.

The interior was magnificent. All the poles that created the structure of the yurt curved up toward a central opening, perhaps twenty feet above our heads, which framed a view of the blue sky. Light filtered down, like a spotlight falling upon the tousled blond hair of Crystal Star, who was sprawled on a fur-draped platform in the center, wearing a magenta silk caftan trimmed with gold braid. The elderly Weimaraner slumbered by her side, his eyes closed. He was in a Sphinx-like position with his paws stretched out, and his head resting on them.

Flint bowed low in front of her, announced us as "Geri Sullivan and her Chihuahua, Pepe," and backed out of the room.

"Have a seat," said Star in a pretty, girlish voice. She waved her hand at a padded red-velvet bench that was in front of the platform. It was very low to the ground, so we had to look up at her. Pepe hopped up to sit by my side.

"Do you know," I asked her, "that there are wild wolves in a pen in the woods?"

Star nodded. "Yes, someone gave them to me.

Poor things. Wolf-dog hybrids. They were going to put them down, but I said we would take them and give them a safe place to live here. If anyone can teach them how to get along with humans, it is Dogawanda."

Pepe gave a soft growl.

"Your little dog has a big heart," said Star.

"It is true," I said, my own heart suddenly swelling with love for my furry companion. He would protect me with his life. I knew that.

"Dogawanda is very interested in your companion," she said. "He senses that he has much to say."

"That is true," I said. For some reason, I didn't feel like elaborating on Pepe's special talents.

"Dogawanda asked me to bring him here to ask him some questions. Will you permit that?"

I nodded.

She nodded as well. "I will now channel Dogawanda, who is inhabiting the body of Max." She stroked the head of the Weimaraner. "Max is ready for retirement. At fourteen, he tires easily, but his indomitable spirit keeps him going. He has been serving as a vessel for Dogawanda for over eleven years. Even when he appears to be asleep, Dogawanda is present in him. The session will end when Dogawanda departs. Of course, I always record these sessions." She reached out and tapped on a tape recorder that sat on a lacquered black table below the platform. I noticed her nails were painted gold. "With your permission, of course."

She didn't wait for my assent. "That is the only way I will know what Dogawanda said."

Star rested her gold-tipped fingers on the head of the slumbering Weimaraner, closed her eyes, and then began swaying gently back and forth. There was silence in the room. I could hear the Weimaraner snoring.

Pepe sneezed. I think the incense was bothering him.

"We should go, Geri," said Pepe. "I do not like the smell of this."

"Hold on a minute," I said. "I just want to see what happens."

Star's eyes suddenly opened wide and she fixed her gaze on Pepe. "Towering Cedar," she said to him, her voice husky, "I, Dogawanda, bid you welcome."

Pepe was startled. "How did he . . . ?" he asked me. "I mean, how did *she* know my made-up name?"

"I didn't tell her," I said, as mystified as my dog. Then I remembered. "Maybe it was Tammy. I think I mentioned your name to her."

"Why do you believe I learned your name from one of the human animals?" Dogawanda asked in a gruff voice. "Dogawanda knows the roots of the trees, the blue of the sky, the cry of the crows. Dogawanda knows all. That is how he knows you are Towering Cedar."

"OK," said Pepe, who seemed at a loss for words. Which was rare for him.

"You are the little dog who has come to teach us

how to be big," Dogawanda intoned. "Now tell me,
Towering Cedar, what is the First Commandment of
the Dog?"

"All roads lead to Dogawanda," said Pepe.

Dogawanda smiled. "Thus you know why you
came hither. All the roads you have ever trod have
brought you to me. You may well be the road that
others follow to my enlightenment."

"I am not a road," said Pepe. "I am a Chihuahua."
He turned to me, puzzled. "It seems she can hear
what I say."

"It is I, Dogawanda, who hears you speak!"
roared Dogawanda. "And do not forget that. As
long as you are faithful to Dogawanda, I will raise
you up to a position of power. Multitudes will come
to listen to your wisdom. You will lead them down
the road less traveled . . ."

"Is that not a line from Robert Frost?" Pepe
asked me.

". . . so by that road," Dogawanda went on,
"others will follow you as you have followed
Dogawanda."

"See, Geri," Pepe said, "I told you that I was your
fortune."

Dogawanda turned his attention to me, or rather
Star did, turning her golden eyes on me.

"You have been given a mighty trust," she said,
"a companion who is blessed with mighty powers,
one who can channel the wisdom of the dog, who
can inspire the adulation of the multitudes. But to
be equal to his talents, you must rise up yourself.

Dogawanda exhorts you to step firmly on the Way of the Dog. My vessel, Crystal Star, can teach you all that you need to know. Otherwise you will be swept off your path, as if by a tsunami."

"Perhaps I should be called Tsunami," said Pepe, sounding proud of himself. "No, I like Towering Cedar better."

"Dogawanda must bid you adieu for now. But think carefully on what I have said. Your destiny is in your hands. And since it is always *now*, know that I am always with you until next we speak. Thus this is *aloha*, not good-bye."

Star let out a gasp and went limp. She stayed slumped over for a long time. I was just thinking I might have to give her CPR when she lifted her head, her whole body quivering and shaking.

"Star, are you OK?" I asked, getting up and going over to her.

"I have never felt such a strong connection," she told me, still shaking but looking radiant, almost beatific. "You will be attending the evening session, won't you?"

"Well . . . ," I started to say.

"We must stay, Geri," Pepe told me. "We can drive back tomorrow. I want to hear more about what Dogawanda says that I say."

"OK," I said.

Star's eyebrows went up. "That's a good sign," she said. "You show much aptitude. I think you would benefit immensely from the training we provide in level two. It teaches you how to think like a dog. You can register for it as soon as you complete the introductory session."

"I can teach you how to think like a dog," said Pepe, "and I will not charge you for it, either. Come to think of it, though, I could use a little extra spending money."

Star came forward and held my hands. "You have a special gift, my dear. You must cultivate it." She pressed a motherly kiss upon my forehead and gathered me into an embrace, which left me smelling like jasmine. "You are truly ready to begin your training, Dogawanda be praised!"

Chapter 11

The evening session went on far into the night, again in the Longhouse, with incense burning constantly. We recited the Seven Commandments of Dogawanda over and over again. Pretty soon it became hypnotic. So hypnotic that I can hardly remember when it ended and we finally got to bed.

I woke up at one point during the night to the howls of the wolf-dogs in the woods. Pepe growled in response. It was a menacing sound, but it made me feel better. I knew he would protect me.

Pepe was up bright and early in the morning and woke me up, chattering about the morning session where he hoped to learn more about himself. We headed over to the lodge for breakfast, which was when I found out that there was no coffee—evidently, caffeine was not part of a Paleolithic diet. I looked around for Tammy, but she was nowhere in sight. Maybe she had the good sense to sleep in.

My head was pounding from the lack of caffeine when we gathered in the Longhouse for the morning session. But a bigger hurt awaited me when Crystal Star appeared onstage and announced that Leaf was missing. She had disappeared during the night.

"I want everyone to form search parties!" Star announced. "It is not like dear Leaf to be absent. If some harm has befallen her, I will never forgive myself!" The Dogawandans fanned out, searching for the missing woman. Artichoke was responsible for assigning people to go in various directions. She sent them out in pairs, like spokes in a wheel, to cover all of the twenty-plus acres that made up the Dogawandan property.

Those of us who were there for the introductory meeting were just supposed to stay in the Longhouse, but Pepe wanted to investigate.

"They are searching the property," Pepe said. "But maybe she just decided to leave. She seemed distressed when she heard about her dog. We should go look for her scent in the parking lot. *Vamanos!*"

"Yes. Maybe she had the good sense to go back to her husband and her dog," I said. "That would certainly be the best for everybody."

We headed out of the Longhouse and down the path toward the front gate and the parking lot. Pepe zigzagged back and forth. "It is strange," he said, "but I do not smell any trace of her in this direction."

The day was already quite warm. The sun was beating down on my pounding head. We passed my beat-up old green Toyota, and I thought how great it would be to get in and just drive away. But then we'd be letting so many people down: Jimmy G, Mark Darling, and Tammy.

"I am catching a scent," said Pepe, "but it is not one I like!" He moved toward the other end of the parking lot where a crude dirt road led up through a grove of trees.

"What?" I asked.

"Follow me, Geri." He trotted up the road and then stopped. I saw that we were on the edge of what seemed to be a construction site. The ground had been leveled and then raked into even plateaus of reddish brown dirt. I could see the bulldozer and backhoe that had done the work parked in the far corner of the big lot. Beyond that was a spectacular view of the valley with the river winding through it.

Pepe lifted his head, sniffing the air. *"Muy malo!"* he said.

"What? What are you smelling?"

"Wait here!" he said. He dashed off toward the bushes on the far side of the lot. I hurried after him. I was not going to let my dog tell me what to do!

When I caught up to him, he was sniffing along the bottom edge of a bank of blackberry brambles that were thick with white blooms. I caught glimpses of color: a brighter green than the leaves, pale white, flashes of red.

"What is it, Pepe?" I asked.

"Something you should not see," he declared. He tried to rush at me to push me back, but I ignored him and crouched down to see what he was looking at. I saw a pale arm, extended, palm up, fingers curled toward the sky. Livid red stripes ran along its length.

She lay twisted and nude upon the ground, her body covered with vivid scratches. Her eyes were closed. Her lips were blue. Her red braid was twisted around her neck.

"It's Tammy!" I said.

"*Sí,*" said Pepe. "*Pobrecita.*"

"She's dead," I said.

"*Sí,* and Fuzzy has lost her human," said Pepe mournfully.

Tears were running down my cheeks. I brushed them aside. I bent down to touch her skin, but it was cold and damp.

"We must notify the authorities," Pepe said.

"Yes, and tell the Dogawandans!"

"They are nearby," said Pepe. "I can hear voices. Call them!"

"Help! Help!" I cried. "Over here! I found her!"

Pepe joined me, giving a few tiny howls.

A few minutes later, we heard crashing in the bushes very near to where we were, and Artichoke came charging through the brambles. Her long dark hair had come loose and was tangled with leaves.

"What is it?" she asked.

I stepped aside and pointed at the body.

"Oh my Dog!" Artichoke shouted, kneeling down and touching Tammy's neck tentatively. She turned to look at us. "She's dead!" She seemed amazed.

"Yes, my dog just found her."

"What happened to her?"

"I don't know." I was surprised she was asking me.

"Perhaps wild animals, maybe a bear," said Artichoke mournfully, bending her head to examine the body more closely. "See the scratch marks all over her?"

"What should we do?" I asked.

"I need to tell Star," Artichoke said. "She will be inconsolable. Every one of her children is precious to her. And someone needs to contact the authorities."

"I'll get my cell phone and call nine-one-one," I said.

Artichoke shook her head. "There's no coverage here. You will have to drive down and tell the sheriff."

"We'll do that. Just tell me where to go." I wanted to get out of there as quickly as possible.

"Fern Lake," said Artichoke. "Right on the main street."

"What is this place?" I asked, turning to go and realizing I needed to be able to identify the location of the body.

"Say she's at the edge of the construction site. Everyone will know where that is."

"Is she safe?" I asked. Then realized how absurd that sounded. "If it's a bear, won't he come back?"

"Perhaps we should leave your dog to guard the body," Artichoke suggested.

"No way, Jose!" said Pepe. "I'm going with Geri!"

"He has to come with me," I said.

Artichoke nodded. "OK. Well, then, hurry!"

As we headed down the road, I heard the wolf-dogs howling.

Chapter 12

The police station was in a small storefront on the main street. I sat on a wooden bench in the lobby with Pepe by my side. A rather large, middle-aged woman wearing beige cat-shaped glasses sat behind the front desk. Her ginger-colored hair had been badly permed. The name plate on her desk said her name was Alice Keyes. She spent most of her time on the phone, talking with one of her friends.

"You'll never guess what happened up at the Dogawanda compound. . . . Yes, I told you those folks were weirdoes. This was bound to happen sooner or later."

Occasionally she put her friend on hold and answered what appeared to be official calls. I could tell she was following the unfolding case up at the retreat center.

"I'll see if I can find Ray and get him up there," she would say.

I could see her eyeing me and my dog with bright eyes, and I'm sure she wanted to get my version of events, but she probably wasn't allowed to question a witness on her own.

Alice cradled the phone between her left ear and shoulder. Evidently she was on hold with someone. She reached into a small wooden bowl on her desk with her free hand and withdrew what looked like a pretzel.

"Can your dog have a treat?" she asked me.

"*Dos, por favor,*" said Pepe, scampering right over to her before I had a chance to answer.

Alice smiled and tossed three pretzels on the floor for him. Pepe snapped them up.

"She gave me *tres,*" said Pepe, scampering over to me. "This *policia senora* is my first cop *amiga.*"

"I've always liked Chihuahuas," said Alice, hanging up the phone. "You want some coffee?" she asked me.

"That would be great," I said. My headache had become a pounding, throbbing vise gripping the top of my head.

As she handed me a Styrofoam cup of coffee, brought in from the back room, I thought I might be able to gain her sympathy. "Thanks," I said. "I really need this. Can you believe? They don't have any coffee up there. I was desperate."

She gave me a faint, slightly predatory smile. Her eyes gleamed behind her glasses.

I took a sip of the coffee. It was strong, like black sludge, but it was exactly what I needed. "I was just up there for the introductory weekend," I said. "Checking it out."

"What did you think?" she asked.

"It was pretty strange," I said. "I don't really understand the philosophy."

"I hear they do weird rituals at night," she said, licking her lips. "Running around in the woods naked. Pretending to be dogs"—she winked at me—"in more ways than one."

Oh, wow! I really missed a lot by going straight to my room. "I didn't see any of that," I confessed. Her smile fell. "But then again, I went to bed early. I don't really know what happened last night."

She brightened again. "Well, something obviously went down." She tapped her finger on the clipboard on her desk. "That poor girl."

"Yes, her name was Tammy Darling," I said.

She perked up. "Really? They're telling me that everyone is calling her Leaf."

"That's the name Dogawanda gave her," I said. "But her real name is Tammy Darling."

"I'll get on the phone and tell the sheriff," she said. As she was dialing, she looked over at me. "So what name did Dogawanda give you?" she asked.

"I don't have a name yet," I said, which suddenly made me sad. I didn't realize it, but I had a sort of yearning to see what Dogawanda would see in me. A tree? A flower? A bird? "But my dog got a name. He's Towering Cedar."

"Well, tell Towering Cedar to get his nose out of there!" she said, pointing to where Pepe was snuffling around the wastebasket. The sheriff must have come on the line then, because I heard her telling him that the victim was Tammy Darling. "The woman you've got waiting here in the office told me." He must have chastised her about talking to me because she said, "Of course not! She volunteered the information."

And that was that. I went back to sipping my syrupy coffee and she called up another friend and began gossiping about the Dogawandans again, starting with the exciting news about the dead body and proceeding to list every wrongdoing associated with them. Apparently they had started building on their property without getting the proper permits. It also sounded like the matter was going to be settled within a few days at a hearing of the Board of Adjustment.

There was a commotion outside. A big SUV with the word SHERIFF printed in gold letters on the side pulled up at the same time as a white van that was emblazoned with the logo of the Dogawanda retreat center—a huge yellow five-pointed star framing the head of a dog. A middle-aged man in a brown uniform got out of the SUV. He also wore a pistol belt, a light-colored cowboy hat, and a shiny silver badge on his chest. A gaggle of green-clothed men and women emerged from the van. I didn't see Star anywhere, but as they filed into the room, I recognized Artichoke. Her hair was still tangled and her clothing rumpled. And walking beside her, supporting her with a hand placed under her elbow, was a woman who looked vaguely familiar. She had long, dark curly hair and a friendly, open face. It was her walk that was most familiar, a sort of languid sway that I instantly recognized but couldn't place.

Pepe's little nose was sniffing the air like crazy. He ran over to her and then ran back to me, sniffing my leg. "She smells just like you," he said. "If you subtract the jasmine and incense. Why is that, Geri?"

The woman stopped about halfway into the room, apparently shocked by the sight of me. I saw her instinctively start to turn around and run. Then she stopped herself.

"Because she is my sister," I said as recognition dawned.

Chapter 13

"Geri?" she said, taking a tentative step toward me.

"Terry?" I said in response.

"No, my name is Flicker," she said impatiently, continuing to gaze on my face as if she were thirsty and I was a drink of cool water.

"But you used to be Terry," I said. "Terry Sullivan."

She shuddered. "Don't ever call me that!" she said. We stared at each other. Her eyes were the greenish blue I remembered, striking against the tanned skin of her face.

"Wow!" said one of the green-clad ones. "You two could be sisters."

"Hush!" said Artichoke. She looked from one of us to the other. "I think they are."

"What are you doing here?" Terry asked.

"I came up for the introductory weekend," I said. "What are you doing here?"

"She's here to be questioned, along with all of

these other folks," said the sheriff. "Now break it up. No talking to each other while waiting to be interviewed. I want to know who was the last person to talk to the victim."

"I spoke to her at lunch," I volunteered. "That was about one p.m." I looked at Terry. "She said she was going to go speak to her spiritual advisor. Someone named Flicker."

"All right!" the sheriff said. "What's your name?" I told him and he wrote it down. "And who saw her after that?"

To my relief, Terry spoke up. "She came to speak to me. I'm her spiritual advisor. My name is Flicker." She looked at me defiantly when she said that. "But she left about three p.m. I thought she was going to talk to Artichoke."

The sheriff rolled his eyes. "And is Artichoke here?"

Artichoke stepped forward. "She never came to see me."

"So it looks like she was waylaid sometime after three p.m. Did anyone see her after that?"

A few people thought they might have seen her heading for the hot springs later that night, but no one was sure it was her. "She seemed to be in a hurry," said one woman. "She had her head down and it was dark. I greeted her, but she didn't respond. Which was unusual. So that's why I couldn't tell for sure if it was her."

"And was there anyone else still at the hot springs when you left?" asked the sheriff.

"Just Fox Black," said the woman. A blush spread across her cheeks and she looked down.

"Well, where is this Fox Black?" asked the sheriff.

"He's on his way," said one of the deputies.

"So unless this Fox Black saw her, you might have been the last one to see her alive," said the sheriff, gazing suspiciously at my sister.

"I think she might have talked to Crystal Star," I said, remembering how Star had known Pepe's Dogawandan name. Either that or there really was an entity named Dogawanda who could discern Pepe's true name.

"Yes, where is Crystal Star?" asked the sheriff impatiently.

"She's on her way in too," said one of the deputies.

"Well, let's begin the questioning," the sheriff said. "You!" He pointed at my sister. "Go with him!" He pointed at one of his deputies. "You!" He pointed at me. "In here!" He gestured toward an office in back of Alice's desk.

I followed him with Pepe trotting behind me. It was a small room, mostly filled by a metal desk that was covered with papers. It actually reminded me a little of Jimmy G's office, minus the aquarium and the smell of old food. This office smelled like old coffee and old paper. The blinds on the tiny window were covered with dust. A calendar featuring a photo of a buck in the woods hung from the wall, along with a number of framed certificates and photos of the sheriff posing beside what I assumed were local celebrities. One shot showed him on the set of *Northern Exposure*, which had been shot in the nearby town of Roslyn.

"My favorite show when I was in high school!" I said when I saw it.

The sheriff did not look amused. He gestured for me to sit down on a wooden chair facing the desk, then plunked himself down in the old green upholstered armchair behind the desk. The springs squeaked as he settled in. He introduced himself as Sheriff Pager, then asked for my contact information.

After writing that down, he wanted to know what I was doing up at the Dogawanda Center. I decided to skip the part about being a PI. For some reason, law enforcement types seemed not to like private investigators, especially ones who weren't licensed or trained.

"I was attending the introductory weekend," I said.

"For what reason?"

"Just curiosity, I guess," I said. "Since I have a dog myself"—I pointed at Pepe, who was sitting quietly by my side—"I wanted to learn about dog wisdom."

"So how did you meet the victim?" he asked.

"I met her in the lunch line," I said. "She seemed nice enough. She told me a little bit about her former life. That's how I learned her name was Tammy Darling. She was married and lived in Seattle."

"So who do you know up there?"

"No one," I said.

"What about that woman who said she was your sister?"

"That is my sister," I said. "But I haven't seen her for over ten years. I had no idea she was involved with the Dogawandans."

"I found her for you!" said Pepe happily.

"That seems unlikely," the sheriff said.

"She disappeared ten years ago when she was twenty," I said. "If you check, you'll see there's a missing persons report. My older sister and I filed it back in 2000. Her name is Terry Sullivan."

"And you've never heard from her since?" he asked suspiciously.

"Not once."

"So you don't know what she's been doing?"

"Well, obviously living with the Dogawandans," I said. I didn't really want to get into Terry's life before she disappeared. It wasn't very savory. The last time we had heard from her, she was dancing at a strip club. Maybe the sheriff would think her lifestyle made her more likely to commit a crime like murder.

He didn't seem convinced but went on. "Tell me what you talked about with the victim."

"You mean Tammy?" For some reason it bugged me that she didn't have a name.

"Tammy."

Another trap I might step into. I kept it light. "She told me about her intention to go on to level three. That would mean she needed to sign up for another class. She was going to talk to her spiritual advisor about making that happen." I hoped that would jibe with what Terry would tell them.

"And her spiritual advisor was your sister?"

"Yes, but I didn't know that at the time," I said. "She called her Flicker."

"Ridiculous!" snorted the sheriff. It was unclear if he was referring to her name or the fact that I didn't know she was there.

"How did Tammy die?" I asked.

"Cannot discuss that," said the sheriff.

"Tell him about the wolves," Pepe suggested.

"Do you know there are wolves up there at the compound?" I asked.

The sheriff seemed taken aback. "What makes you say that?"

Well, I couldn't really tell him my dog told me to say that. "Just thought it might be important."

The sheriff's eyebrows rose. "We do know about the wolves," he said carefully. "The townsfolk don't like it much. Think they might get loose and attack someone."

"Like Tammy?" I asked.

His eyes narrowed.

"What would make you think she was attacked by wolves?" he asked.

"She had what looked like claw marks on her arm," I said. "But Artichoke thought she might have been attacked by a bear."

The sheriff snorted again. "Bears don't attack

humans. Not in these woods anyway." But he made another note.

Just then, Alice poked her head back in. "Crystal Star has arrived," she said, "and Fox Black is with her." Even Alice seemed to be affected by the presence of the rock star. I could hear the excitement in her voice.

Chapter 14

The outer room was abuzz with the presence of Crystal Star. She seemed to be unaffected by the news of Tammy's death. She smiled upon her assembled acolytes and the few townspeople who had come to gawk at the freak show. She was in full regalia, wearing a royal purple silk caftan, her hair pulled up and circled by a gauzy purple scarf. She hung on the arm of Fox Black, who was barefoot, wearing a pair of tight black leather pants, a black T-shirt, and dark glasses.

"Miz Star," said the sheriff. "Could you follow me, please?"

She sailed off with him, with one last glance at Fox Black, who seemed rather lost. All of the women kept their distance from him, even the one who had blushed when she spoke of being the last one in the hot springs with him.

I marched right up to him. "So did you see Leaf last night?" I asked. "Maybe at the hot springs?"

"I don't know," he said. "One naked woman looks kinda like another. In the dark anyway."

Pepe growled at him, an appropriate response, I thought.

"Hey, no talking," said Alice, looking up from her phone call.

I wondered if they had notified Mark of his wife's death yet. Just then the deputy came out from an interview room with my sister. "You're free to go for now," he told her, "but we may have more questions later."

"Let's talk, Terry," I said, grabbing her by the elbow and pulling her outside. The main street, which was lined with tall wooden false-front buildings with wide front porches, looked just like the town in *Northern Exposure*. At one corner was a brick building that housed the bank and across the street to the left was a long low diner. Golden letters in an arc on the dusty plate-glass front window spelled out the name SIT AND GAB.

So that's what we did. It was a quaint little place with knotty pine paneling on the walls and green Naugahyde-upholstered booths along the sides. Various taxidermy animals—squirrels, skunks, owls—stood on little sconces that lined the walls.

The place was pretty packed. I think the news of the suspicious death had traveled rapidly, thanks to Alice and her phone work, and all heads turned when we walked in. I put Pepe in my purse, since I know dogs aren't allowed in eating establishments. Luckily the hostess seated us in the one unoccupied booth at the back of the restaurant, since everyone else wanted to be up close to watch the drama across the street unfold. If only they knew it was unfolding between me and my sister.

There was a stuffed skunk lifting his tail on one side of the booth and a big snowy owl on the other side. Pepe wrinkled his nose when he saw the skunk but cowered at the sight of the owl.

"Where do you get all the animals from?" I asked our waitress, a young woman with a purple streak in her hair and a diamond in her nose.

"The local vet has a sideline in taxidermy," she replied. "Some folks ask him to stuff their pets when they die."

"¡*Ay caramba!*" said Pepe. I had never seen him so upset. He started shaking and his little eyes seemed like they might pop right out of his head.

"Don't worry, Pepe. I won't stuff you," I said to him.

"That would be a fate worse than death," Pepe declared. I did not point out the obvious to him.

I ordered a coffee and a piece of cherry pie. Terry ordered a hot fudge sundae.

"Are you kidding?" I said. "That's not on the Pale-olithic diet!"

She laughed. "Sometimes it's good to be bad."

"What happened to you?" I didn't want to beat around the bush.

"They asked me some questions and I answered them," she said.

"No, I don't mean now. I mean back then!"

The waitress returned with my coffee and pie and Terry's sundae. She dug in with gusto.

"Geri," she said, "I wish I could tell you, but I just can't talk about it."

"What do you mean you can't talk about it?" I asked. "Do you realize what it was like for us?" I stabbed my fork deep into the cherry pie. "We thought you were dead, Terry!" My eyes welled with tears.

Terry reached across the table and put her hand over mine and squeezed it. "Geri, believe me, if I could have told you where I was, I would have. But I couldn't." She licked the chocolate sauce off her spoon. "I wanted to contact you so badly." She plunged the spoon back into the gooey sundae. "Does your dog like ice cream?"

"How thoughtful!" said Pepe, creeping out of the purse and approaching her. "Tell her I love ice cream."

"Wow! I could swear I heard him say he loves ice cream," she said, smiling down at him. She scooped up some of the vanilla and held it out to him. His long pink tongue flicked out and he began polishing off the ice cream.

"Did you really hear him?" I asked. I was a bit jealous. First Star could hear my dog, now my sister! Maybe the Dogawandans did have an uncanny ability to tap into a dog's mind.

"You're kidding, right?" Terry said with a laugh. "It's his attitude. He's so expressive, you can almost imagine what he's thinking."

"During all that time you couldn't have called one of us? Or sent us an e-mail?"

"We don't have access to the outside world," Terry said. "We're really sheltered up there. And that's what I needed."

"You could have come into town and called. Or written a letter," I said.

"Believe me, I was trying to protect you and Cheryl," Terry said, her voice suddenly very serious.

"How long have you been a Dogawandan?" I asked.

"About six years," she said. "I needed to change my life, and it seemed the perfect opportunity. A new name. A new start. Plus it gave me a sense of being part of a family. . . ." Her voice trailed off.

I looked at her. She looked at me.

"I'm sorry, Geri. I'm really sorry," she said. I was still poking at my cherry pie. Terry reached across the table and grabbed my hands. "And I'm happy, really I am, that I got a chance to see you. Even if it messes up my life."

"What do you mean?" I asked.

"Well, I'll have to leave now . . ."

"Why would you have to leave?"

There was a commotion at the door to the restaurant. I twisted around to see the sheriff and a deputy approaching. They had their hands on their guns. They spoke to the hostess, and she pointed back at our table. I quickly grabbed Pepe and stuffed him into my purse. I don't know what

I was thinking. That maybe they were coming to arrest me for having a dog in a restaurant.

They marched over to our table.

"Stand up!" the sheriff said, addressing my sister.

"What is this about?" she asked as she complied with their request.

"Hands behind your back," said the deputy.

"What is going on?" I asked.

"You're under arrest," said the sheriff, clicking a pair of handcuffs around my sister's wrists.

"What for?"

"We ran your name. You've got a warrant."

She looked at me with horror in her eyes. "You told them my real name?"

I held out my hands. "I thought I was helping."

Terry rolled her eyes. "Please don't say anything more about me to anyone!"

Chapter 15

I paid the bill and went back to the police station, but they wouldn't let me anywhere near my sister. The most I could get out of Alice was that they were processing her and would hold her overnight.

I finally called Jimmy G and asked him what I should do. He recommended heading back to Seattle so we could hash things out. So that's what we did. It was a long hot drive. Pepe slept through most of it while I tried to deal with the sense of queasiness and panic I felt about Tammy's death and my sister's arrest. A bigger shock awaited me when we walked into Jimmy G's office.

The usual chaos had been tripled. There were empty boxes all over the floor and the desk, and Jimmy G was trying to cram his prized green-shaded lamp into one of them. The file cabinet drawers were open and empty. Piles of manila folders sat on top of the two waiting room chairs.

"Oh, hey there," said our boss, looking up.

"Hey, yourself," I said.

"And you, little rat-dog," he said to Pepe. "How's it hanging?"

"Bigger than yours," Pepe told him.

Our boss frowned. "Jimmy G could swear he heard a note of sarcasm from your rat-dog," he told me. "That couldn't be possible, could it?"

"Of course not," I said.

"You bet!" said Pepe.

Jimmy G gave up on the lamp and left it sticking half out of the box. "Well," he said, reaching into his ashtray and sticking a short, burned out cigar butt into his mouth. "Maybe Jimmy G's been keeping company with you for too long. You always act like your dog's talking to you, and could be that's just rubbing off on Jimmy G."

I changed the subject. "What's up, boss? Why are you packing?"

"Figure Jimmy G has got to get his stuff out of here before the landlord throws it out on the street," he said. "I just don't see how I can get my hands on the kind of moola I need to pay the rent."

I was pretty sure he was going to ask me for a loan, so I changed the subject. "So how do you want me to proceed with the Mark Darling case?"

"Oh, hey! Got your thinking cap on, doll!" Jimmy G said. "He owes us the balance on his account. Maybe that'll keep the wolf away from the door for at least another month."

"What happened to the deposit?" I asked.

"What deposit?" Jimmy G asked. "You should have collected that when you did the initial interview."

I shook my head. "You didn't mention that." And frankly, neither did *The Private Detective's Bible*, my handy guide to my new profession.

"Does Jimmy G have to tell you everything?" he asked.

"Well, yes, you're training us," I said. "But do you really think we should be collecting money from him under the circumstances?" I asked.

"You delivered the message, right?" Jimmy G asked.

"Yes!"

"That's great. Now go collect the money."

"I'm not sure I can do that, Jimmy G." I really didn't think it was appropriate. Or civilized.

"Part of the job. Got to get used to it. Didn't you say you once worked for a collection agency?"

"Yes, but I wasn't good at it. Anyway, that's not the problem. The problem is that shortly after I delivered the message, Tammy died."

"Died like in dead?"

"Yes, dead." I explained the situation to him, but I left out the part about my sister. It just didn't seem relevant.

"Well, that is unfortunate," said Jimmy G, "but you still did your part of the job."

"Yes, but I can't go ask a man who just lost his wife to give us the money for delivering a message to her hours before her death."

"Well, if you can't do it, Jimmy G can," said my boss. "Come with me, doll, and Jimmy G will show you how it's done."

The man who opened the door looked almost exactly the same as the man we had met almost two days earlier. It shook me up a bit; I expected maybe red eyes or a disheveled appearance.

Maybe he didn't know his wife was dead? I cringed at the thought of being the one to deliver the news. Not Jimmy G.

"So, man," he said, barging into the hall, "so sorry about your loss." In an aside to me, he said, "Important to gain access to the home when collecting a debt."

Mark looked startled but stepped aside to let us parade by, then shut the door behind us. Jimmy G headed straight for the living room and plopped down on a caramel-colored leather couch, which made a slight squeaking sound. I paused on the threshold. Something was off. Something was different, but I couldn't put my finger on it.

"Where's Fuzzy?" said Pepe, looking around the room.

"Yes, where's Fuzzy?" I asked.

"Funniest thing," said Mark, punctuating this statement with a mirthless laugh. "Took off the other night around midnight. Scratched at the door until I let her out. Haven't seen her since."

"A brave *perro*," said Pepe. "No doubt going to the rescue of her companion."

"Did you report her missing?" I asked. "Call the shelter?"

"Geri, focus," said Jimmy G. "There's much more going on here than a missing dog. The man's wife is dead." He turned to Mark. "What have the police told you?" He patted the seat beside him, and when I sat down, he leaned over and said in what he thought was a sotto voce voice, "Always put the client at ease. Make conversation."

I hardly thought that talking about his wife's death would put Mark at ease, but to my surprise it worked. Mark was eager to talk. He stood in front of the fireplace, his elbow on the mantel, facing Jimmy G.

"They told me they think she wandered into the woods at night and was killed by a wild animal, possibly a bear!"

"Aha!" said Pepe.

"That sucks, pal," said Jimmy G. "Did they tell you anything more?"

Mark frowned. "No, they were very cagey. Insisted I should drive over there to talk to them. I was just leaving."

"Are you sure you're in shape to go?" I asked. "Don't you have anyone to drive you?"

"No," said Mark, waving away my concern. "As you recall"—his tone was bitter—"my wife was already dead to me. All that's changed is that she's really dead now." He paused and looked at me suspiciously. "Did you ever deliver my message?"

"Of course we did," I said.

"And?" Mark looked eager for the first time.

"She said she really missed you."

"And Fuzzy! Don't forget Fuzzy!" said Pepe.

"She wanted to come home, but she believed she had to go through another level of training before it would be safe for her to return. And in order to do that, she had to make another payment."

"I knew it!" said Mark, turning away, teeth clenched. "They were just after our money!"

"She looked good. She looked happy," I said. Mark was facing away, so I couldn't see his reaction.

"So you see," said Jimmy G, getting up and going over to Mark. Although not tall, Jimmy G had at least two inches on Mark. "We've come to collect our fee."

Chapter 16

"You've got a lot of nerve!" said Mark, whirling around, his fists clenched. "My wife is dead and you're asking me for money."

"Hey!" said our boss, putting out his hands in a placating gesture. "My operatives"—Jimmy G gestured at me and Pepe—"they are just trainees and so they neglected to collect the deposit on the first visit. According to our standard terms, you must pay half of our fee in advance and the other half upon completion. Seems to Jimmy G you owe us one thousand smackeroos."

"How do I know they actually completed the task?" asked Mark.

I wondered about his anger. Easier to get mad than sad. My sister Terry had always been angry after our parents died. "And what do you mean *trainees*? I wanted licensed PIs. I need them to testify in court."

"What do you mean testify in court?" I asked. The idea both thrilled and terrified me.

"Geri, did I ever tell you about my day in court?" asked Pepe. "I was the expert witness in a case of dog-food tampering."

"Hush, Pepe," I said.

"I've filed a suit against Crystal Star," Mark said. "For alienation of affection and fraud. And now I'm going to add wrongful death. I don't know how, but I know they were responsible."

"All the more reason to pay our fee," said Jimmy G, taking a step closer to Mark. "You can keep us on retainer for an additional five hundred dollars."

"Look!" said Mark. He pushed his hands toward Jimmy G but without actually touching him. "I'm suing for a half a million. My lawyer thinks we have a good case. I'll pay your agency a commission. Ten percent of whatever I get. After legal costs, of course. As long as your associates continue to gather evidence on my behalf. That's one option."

Jimmy G looked thoughtful. "And the other?"

"I'll write you a check for one thousand right now. Of course, I still intend to subpoena your"— he narrowed his eyes and squinted at me—"operatives, as you call them. But"—he pointed his finger at me—"she better be licensed by then!"

The phone began to ring. Mark frowned, then headed out into the hallway to answer it. I wondered if it was a sympathy call. I wondered if he had told anyone about his wife's death. His voice was too low to hear what he was saying.

Jimmy G sat down again, leaned back, and crossed his legs. He seemed pretty proud of himself. "See how it's done, doll?" he asked.

Mark slammed down the phone and reentered the living room. He was obviously shaken. His face was pale, his eyes frozen.

"That was the county sheriff," he said.

I nodded. "Sheriff Pager," I said.

Mark gave me a sharp look. "Yes, Sheriff Pager. He says my wife was murdered." He threw the word at me like an accusation.

I was taken aback. "Really? Murdered?"

"Yes, the good news is that they already have a suspect in custody."

"No!" I said, thinking of my sister.

Mark looked at me with narrowed eyes. "Did you know this?"

I shook my head, momentarily unable to speak.

"Tell you what we'll do," said Jimmy G, going over to Mark and draping his arm around the other man's shoulders. "My operatives here will go back up there and investigate this murder."

"Sounds like the sheriff already has it wrapped up," said Mark.

"Can't be too careful," said Jimmy G. "My associates have an inside track. Sheriff doesn't have that."

Mark looked uncertain.

"Of course, we'll have to charge extra," Jimmy G

said. "For hazard pay. Can't be sending my operatives into danger without additional compensation."

"How about twelve percent commission on the
settlement?" asked Mark.

"Fifteen percent," countered Jimmy G.

They finally settled at fourteen percent.

As we walked away from the house, I said to
Jimmy G, "We came here to get one thousand dollars
and we're leaving with nothing but a promise. I
don't see how that was so effective."

"Hey," said my boss, "we came here to get one
thousand dollars and we're leaving with the potential of making . . ." He paused and scratched his
head. "What's fourteen percent of one million?"

"It's a gamble, boss. That's what it is. And the
odds are against us," I said as we piled into Jimmy
G's car, a red Thunderbird convertible from the
sixties.

"Those are the kind of odds that Jimmy G likes,"
he said as he revved up the engine. It sounded like
it needed a muffler. "You don't get the big payoffs
without some risks."

"No wonder he is broke," Pepe said.

"So you gotta get yourself back up to that cult
and start digging," Jimmy G said as he pulled into
traffic.

"I am good at digging," said Pepe.

"You don't have a problem with that, do you?"
Jimmy G asked me. Before I could answer, he said,
"Sure, they're a bunch of weirdoes and it could be
dangerous—Jimmy G knows that. But that's the

nature of the private dick business. Sometimes you just gotta put your neck on the line."

"*Sí*. Our necks, not *his*," said Pepe.

"No problem, boss," I said. "We want to catch whoever did it as badly as anybody."

"*We?*" asked the boss, glancing over at me. Pepe was sitting on my lap. "Oh, yeah, you and the rat-dog. He's a regular Sherlock Chihuahua."

"You would make a terrible Watson," Pepe told Jimmy G.

"OK," I said. "We'll head back up there first thing tomorrow." I wanted to find out what I could about Terry. Was she the suspect?

"Copacetic," said my boss. "Jimmy G will come up, too. Establish a base camp so you can make regular reports."

"I hope we don't have to join the cult, though."

"What? Are you nuts?"

"The introductory weekend is almost over," I explained. "If we can't figure out who killed Tammy by tomorrow night, we might have to join the Dogawandans to stay at the Center after that."

"Oh," said Jimmy G. "Do what you have to. Just don't start believing you have to worship a dog."

"She already does," Pepe told him. "*Moi.*"

Chapter 17

"It can't be my sister!" I said to Pepe as we were driving home. "It can't be my sister!"

Pepe said nothing, which was highly unusual.

"You think she did it?" I asked him.

"I do not know your sister," he said.

"But you know me," I pointed out.

"That is not to know your sister," he said. "I do not know my siblings."

"You had siblings?" I asked.

"Of course. I was the youngest of a litter of five."

"I didn't know that, Pepe. You never talk about your family."

"That is because I was taken away from them when I was only six weeks old." He seemed sad as he spoke.

"Oh, I'm so sorry!" I said. Then I thought about my own family story, which was also full of abandonment and loss. My parents had died in a car accident when I was sixteen, and my younger sister had been kicked out by my big sister three years later when she was seventeen and disappeared altogether three years later. Although we live only about twenty miles apart, I'm not close to my big sister, Cheryl. Still I got an immediate urge to see her, if for no other reason than to let her know about Terry.

Instead of driving home, I headed for the floating bridge. Its official name is the Governor Albert D. Rosellini Bridge—Evergreen Point, but everyone just calls it the floating bridge. And it's the longest floating bridge on earth. Two high-rise sections connect the bridge to land, but the middle section lies just above the surface of Lake Washington. You can look out as you fly along (or crawl if it's rush hour). On the south side, the dark blue lake water is calm and glassy, and on the northern side it's usually choppy, with little peaks of white on the tops of the waves.

My sister and her husband live in the Issaquah Highlands, a once-rural area rapidly being covered by developments, just east of Bellevue, Seattle's little sister of a town. Bellevue tries hard to look glamorous and grown-up with its office towers and shopping malls, but it's smaller and less cosmopolitan than downtown Seattle.

Cheryl lives in a development called Stonybrook, where all the streets are curved in on themselves and all the huge three-story houses are crammed into tiny lots with only a few feet between them.

Cheryl's house looks just like its neighbors, up to the basket of purple petunias dangling from a pot on the porch. I pulled into the driveway behind my sister's silver minivan, which displayed a BABY ON BOARD bumper sticker. The baby was now eighteen months old and having a screaming, squalling meltdown, judging by the sounds we heard when we got out of the car. Pepe began shivering. He is not afraid of much, but he is afraid of children.

"Oh my ears! My delicate ears!" he said.

"You can stay in the car," I told him. I knew my sister did not want a dog in her house.

"But no, I have a job to do, and so I must do my duty," said Pepe, marching by my side up the front steps.

I was surprised Cheryl could hear the doorbell what with all the yelling going on inside, but she answered the door with D.J. hitched up on her hip. His face was bright red and his cheeks were covered with snot. But as soon as he saw Pepe, his eyes widened and his screams stopped.

"Doggie!" he chortled, holding out his slime-covered little fingers.

"Well, your dog is making himself useful for once," Cheryl said. She set D.J. down on his wobbly feet (he had just started walking at eighteen months—Cheryl carried him everywhere, so there was really no reason for him to learn). He lunged for Pepe, who darted behind me.

"Let him pet the dog!" said Cheryl.

"He might hurt him!" I snatched Pepe up into my arms.

"You're right!" said Cheryl. "Your dog has sharp teeth."

"Doggie!" wailed D.J., throwing himself at my legs and attempting to climb up me.

"Be nice to your auntie Geri," said Cheryl, trying to detach D.J. from me, but he clung like a little monkey while Pepe shivered in my arms.

"Speaking of aunts," I said in a bright voice, even though I doubted D.J. could hear me over his ear-splitting shrieks, "I just found Auntie Terry."

But Cheryl heard me. "What?"

"I found Terry," I said, with some pride.

"I found her," said Pepe.

Cheryl frowned. "D.J., let go this minute! Or I'll put you in a time-out!" She tried to pry him off me, but he just held on tighter.

"OK, you are now in a time-out!" said Cheryl. She unlatched his fingers from me, one finger at a time and carried him away down the hall, howling and kicking and hitting. Even when she closed the door to his room, I could still hear him shrieking.

While Cheryl tried to quiet D.J., I stood in the living room and looked at the framed photos displayed on the mantel over the glassed-in fake fireplace. Photos of D.J. and his big sister, Danielle. Danielle posing with her chubby chin propped on interlaced hands. D.J. clutching a bright blue bear. Also on the mantel, photos of Cheryl and her husband, Don (I call him Don the Dentist). The wedding party: including me as bridesmaid (in an awful baby blue chiffon gown) and Jeff, my ex-husband, on the groom's side, looking ever so handsome with his slightly shaggy hair and dark blue velvet sports coat. A little farther along, our wedding, which took place a year later, with Cheryl as my maid of honor and Don as Jeff's best man. Terry was already gone when Cheryl got married, so she didn't appear in these photos.

While I was looking at the photos, my cell phone buzzed and I saw that Felix was calling. But just then, Cheryl came back into the room.

"Do you have any photos of Terry?" I asked her.

"Somewhere," she said. "I don't put them out. I don't want to try to explain who she is to the kids." I knew my sister disapproved of Terry's lifestyle (what we knew of it). And she also felt guilty. After our parents died, she had to be a guardian and mother figure for us. When Terry went wild, Cheryl, applied the advice she got from parenting experts at the time and threw her out of the house. Terry never forgave her for that. No wonder Cheryl was so overindulgent with her own kids.

"Where's your dog?" she asked.

I hadn't even noticed he was gone. "Probably in the kitchen," I said. Pepe is very impressed with Cheryl's cooking, since she cooks American classics like meat loaf and roast beef.

Sure enough, he was sitting in the middle of the floor, staring up at the granite counters, his little nose sniffing away. I could see what caught his attention: a plate of home-baked chocolate chip cookies. They gave off a delicious aroma.

"Might as well have a snack," said Cheryl. I could still hear D.J. wailing in the background. She opened the refrigerator and took out a carton of milk and poured us each a glass. She put out two sunflower plates on the round glass-topped table set into an alcove off the kitchen, brought over the plate of cookies, and motioned for me to sit down. Pepe pawed at my legs, wanting me to pick him up and put him on my lap but I ignored him.

"So what's the news about Terry?" Cheryl asked as she came over to the table with the glasses of milk. "Did you find her online?" She knew that I had been searching for Terry for years.

"No, I saw her in person!" I said.

"You're kidding?" Cheryl sat down with a thump. "Where?"

"At a ranch out near Cle Elum," I said.

"What were you doing there?"

"I was working a case," I said. I helped myself to a cookie, broke off a piece, checked to make sure there were no chocolate chips in it, and held it out to Pepe under the table. He immediately carried it out onto the kitchen floor, where he sat down to polish it off with gusto.

Cheryl frowned. "So you still think you're a private detective?"

Cheryl didn't think too much of my new profession. She didn't approve of my being an artist either, which is why I dropped out of college, abandoning my art degree for interior design (more practical). To be fair, it was also because I needed to support my new husband, who was getting his MBA. Cheryl also didn't approve of our divorce, but there wasn't much she could do about that.

"I *am* a private detective," I said, "or to be more precise, I'm training to be a private detective. And my assignment was to go undercover in this cult—"

"That sounds really dangerous," Cheryl said.

"Not with me at her side," said Pepe, licking his lips.

"Cheryl, I'm trying to tell you about Terry!"

"Yes, yes, go on. I'm listening."

"She belongs to the cult. She's got a new name."

"What?"

"She goes by Flicker."

"What kind of name is that?"

"They all have names like that. Leaf. Flint. Fox. Artichoke."

"What kind of cult is this?"

"The Dogawandans."

"Never heard of them."

"They worship an ancient warrior spirit who talks through a dog. Or maybe it's an ancient warrior dog. I'm not quite sure."

"I think Dogawanda is a dog, for sure," said Pepe. "His wisdom is that of a *perro*."

"Geri, you're making that up."

"No, I'm not!"

"That sounds ridiculous!"

"Actually it makes some kind of sense when you're there."

"It's not ridiculous at all," said Pepe. "Everyone should listen to dogs."

"So did Terry explain what she's been doing all these years?" Cheryl asked. "Why she hasn't contacted us?"

"No, not really. She told me she couldn't tell me. She said she was trying to protect us."

"Probably just trying to protect us from knowing what she was really up to," said Cheryl. Terry had been running with a rough crowd right around the time she disappeared.

"I suppose it's possible she went to jail," I said. "Maybe she didn't want to tell us. She did mention needing to make a fresh start."

"Perhaps she is a fugitive," said Pepe, "and that is why the police came for her. Like Corinna in *Paraiso Perdido*. She was living under a false name . . ."

"This is not one of your Spanish soap operas!" I said.

"It sounds exactly like *Paraiso Perdido*," said Cheryl.

Really? Did everyone watch telenovelas except me?

"Corinna came back to town but would not

explain where she was for the last ten years," Cheryl said.

"Maybe she has amnesia," suggested Pepe, "like Corinna's sister, Lourdes."

"What's next?" asked Cheryl. "When do I get to see her?"

"That might be a little difficult," I said. "She's under arrest at the moment."

"What?"

"Yes, while we were there, we found a dead body—"

"This is exactly why you must stop working as a private detective!" Cheryl declared. Well, she might be able to order her husband and kids around, but she couldn't boss me anymore. I decided to ignore her as I had in the past.

"—and it seems that the sheriff thinks Terry did it!"

"For all you know, she had been in prison the past ten years, like Corinna," Cheryl said.

"A good point!" Pepe declared. "Or perhaps she has traumatic amnesia, like Lourdes. She was traumatized because she believed she had committed a murder. Only she had really been framed but she didn't know that."

"Come on, Cheryl," I said. "She's our sister. She's not a murderer."

"We don't know anything about her and what she's done in the past," Cheryl pointed out.

There was some truth to that.

"I'll find out," I said.

"Yes, this is a case for Sullivan and Sullivan!" said Pepe, referring to the name of the fictional detective agency he thinks we are running.

"I'm heading back up there tomorrow," I said. "I'll figure out what's going on and let you know."

"OK, Geri," said Cheryl with a sigh. "But please be careful. You don't know what's going on. I can't afford to lose another sister!"

Chapter 18

I cried on the way home from Cheryl's. I couldn't believe that she seemed so willing to believe the worst of Terry. Or that she was so dismissive of my skills as a detective. I had dreamed for years about reuniting my splintered family, and now it seemed that finding Terry might push us farther apart.

"Geri," said Pepe as we crossed back over the floating bridge, "I am sorry you are sad, but I do not understand why."

"Well, I just want both of my sisters back in my life."

"So it is important to you to be close to your siblings?"

"Well, yes!"

"You do not believe, as Dogawanda does, that you must make your own pack?"

"Pepe, that stuff is silly."

"I do not know. I have not seen my siblings for many moons."

I blinked. Since when did Pepe speak like a movie Indian or a New Age guru? Oh, maybe since we met a New Age guru!

"Does that bother you?" I asked him.

"No, I have made my own pack and I am happy."

"Who is in your pack, Pepe?" I asked as I turned off on the curving off-ramp that would take me home.

"Just you."

"Then how much of a pack is it?"

"We can adopt others. I have not found the proper compadres yet."

"Jimmy G?"

"Too *estupido*."

"Brad?" I named my best friend who runs a little antique shop.

"No, he stuffs animals." Pepe hates the taxidermy animals that Brad collects.

"Albert?"

"Are you *loco*? A cat cannot be part of a dog pack."

"What about Felix?"

In answer to that, Pepe just snorted and turned his head away.

Speaking of Felix, I realized I had not checked his message. I pulled over, fished my phone out of my purse, and dialed voice mail.

"Geri, I'm thinking of you and wishing you were here," he said. "We're filming at Sandpoint, probably until late tonight. If you get this message, you should come by. Warehouse thirteen."

Wow! Just what I needed to take my mind off my troubles. I was curious to see how a movie set might be different from the sets on *Dancing with Dogs*, the reality TV show in which Pepe and I had participated a month earlier. And Sandpoint was just a few minutes away.

Sandpoint is the name for the old naval air station that was abandoned in the late 1950s. I've always loved it. There is something about abandoned buildings that intrigues me. The lives lived there. The melancholy that hangs over them. The three-story brick barracks are all boarded up, and that makes me sad. I imagine they are not earthquake safe, but I think of how many people they could house, considering how many homeless people have to sleep on the streets every night in Seattle.

But the huge hangars have been converted to various uses. The University of Washington uses one for their purchasing department. And the Seattle Public Library leases another to store all the books donated for their semiannual book sales. On the days of the sale, the warehouse is filled with long tables, each one lined with books, and people shuffle up and down, craning their neck to look at titles, filling boxes and shopping carts and bags with their finds.

The rest of the grounds have been converted to various uses, including a rock-climbing wall, a marsh restoration area with trails, a big community garden, and an off-leash area for dogs. I pointed this out to Pepe as we drove through the front gate and past the closed stand where a guard used to check credentials.

"I do not need permission to go off-leash," he said. "But if there is a food vendor, I would visit them."

"Well, if this is anything like the *Dancing with Dogs* set, they'll have a craft service," I said as I pulled into a parking space in front of warehouse thirteen, right behind a truck that read NORTHWEST LIGHTS AND SOUND.

The large loading doors on the side of the warehouse were open. The space inside was dim and filled with equipment and people. We spotted the craft table right inside the door. Coffee urns and Styrofoam cups. A plastic tub full of ice and plastic water bottles and cans of pop. Platters of sliced cheese and lunch meats. Pepe was prancing around on his hind legs, trying to get the attention of the bored girl sitting behind the table, who was talking on her cell phone. Pepe's nose didn't quite clear the table, so she couldn't see him. I went over and helped myself to a paper plate and some cheese and ham, then set it on the ground in front of Pepe.

The center of the warehouse was occupied by a mock-up of the inside of a cabin, with a kitchen, a bedroom, and a living room arranged side by side. Fake trunks of trees were visible through the windows. It was designed to look like a summer cabin, down to the Reader's Digest Condensed Books on the shelves. I wondered for a minute if I could get a job creating sets. That would be a perfect transition from staging and possibly more fun, or at least more lucrative, than being a private detective.

At the moment, nothing was being filmed. The big cameras were unmanned. A knot of people stood in the center of the room, talking and gesticulating. One woman carried a clipboard. A guy I assumed was the director sported a backward-facing baseball cap and a sports coat. Chloe was in their midst, wrapped in a pink chenille bathrobe. Felix must have spotted me when I came in because suddenly he was at my side, giving me a big hug.

"So glad you came, Geri!" he said. "Let me show you around."

But just then, the director shouted, "OK, everyone! We're ready to shoot." The room came alive. All the guys who had been standing around drinking coffee or who were standing outside smoking, came pouring back in and began tinkering with lights and moving cameras. Chloe stood in the center of the set, still wearing the bathrobe and shivering.

The lights came up, but somehow they made it look like it was night in the cabin. One lamp glowed orange. Orange like the eyes of a wolf.

The cameras began moving, zooming in on Chloe, who positioned herself by the door. The woman with the clipboard approached her and held out her hand. Chloe stripped off the bathrobe and handed it to her. She was nude, and her body was covered with long red stripes, the stripes of claws, the stripes I had last seen on Tammy's arm.

"Action!" said the director, and the cameras began filming as Chloe pretended to be terrified. Her eyes wide, she pressed her nude body against the door while someone else thumped and rattled the doorknob on the other side. I couldn't take it and turned abruptly and left.

"What is it, Geri?" Felix had come after me.

"She just looked so much like Tammy," I said between big messy sobs. Felix led me over to a picnic table set up on the lawn of a nearby building, and it all spilled out: the weirdness of the Dogawandans, the strange encounter with Crystal Star, the finding of Tammy's body, the unexpected meeting with my sister, my guilt about causing her arrest, and the upsetting conversation with Mark. Felix sat beside me, murmured sympathetically at every twist and turn of my story, and went to fetch some napkins so I could wipe my teary face.

Finally I remembered that I was interrupting Felix at work.

"Don't you have to be in there?" I asked.

"No," he said with a grimace. "We lost the dogs."

"I am not lost," said Pepe, who had jumped up into my lap.

"You lost the dogs? As in they're running loose somewhere?"

"No, the animal shelter took them away. You know, those wolf-hybrids are considered dangerous and any sign of neglect is taken quite seriously. Apparently they broke through a fence and were roaming the neighborhood. Could have killed a small child easily. You just never know what a wolf-hybrid is going to do."

"Or a small dog," I said with a shiver, hugging Pepe tight. "What do you mean what a wolf-hybrid is going to do?"

"When you mate a wolf with a dog, you get an animal that's fifty percent wolf and fifty percent dog. Most people think it's the wolf that's dangerous. But actually it's the dog. Wolves tend to be timid around people and will run away when they feel threatened, but dogs are more likely to be aggressive, to people and other dogs. Combine that with the powerful jaws of a wolf and you've got trouble. A wolf-hybrid is sort of like a gun. You don't know when it's going to go off. Maybe never. Maybe tomorrow."

"So what are you going to do?"

"We've got to find someone else who has hybrids, and that's going to be hard. Because they have such a bad reputation, many owners of hybrids conceal the dog's true background. They'll claim it's a husky or shepherd mix."

"I know where you can find two wolf-hybrids," I said.

"Really?"

"Yes! Pepe discovered them in the woods at the

Dogawanda compound. They were in a big pen behind an electrified fence."

"I told them who was boss!" said Pepe.

"I asked Crystal Star about them and she said someone gave them to her. She thinks she can get Dogawanda to teach them how to behave."

"Or me," said Pepe. "Did you tell Felix how I am going to be the next Dogawanda?"

"Or Pepe!" I said. "He thinks he can communicate with them."

"I can!" said Pepe with an indignant tone in his voice. "Because a little wolf remains in all dogs."

"Oh, that sounds dangerous," said Felix.

"I beg to differ," said Pepe.

"Unless she has some sort of training, she could be in real jeopardy."

"Oh, he is referring to Star, not me," said Pepe. "He knows I can handle those wolves."

"Well, maybe you can teach her how to work with them," I said. "And at the same time ask if you can borrow them for the filming."

"What a great idea!" said Felix. "Do you think Crystal Star will be open to that?"

"Well, we do seem to have her interest," I said. "Or at least Pepe does."

"She sees my potential," said Pepe.

"Why don't you come along?" I asked. "We're heading back up there tomorrow."

Chapter 19

"This is Felix Navarro," I said to the green-clad acolyte who guarded the entrance to the Dogawandan compound. "The famous Wolf Whisperer."

"Really?" said the man. He had a bushy beard and long dark hair. His name tag said his name was Kale.

"Yes. And I'm sure Star will want to talk to him. He can help her with her wolves."

We had pulled into the dusty parking lot of the Dogawanda compound around noon on Sunday, and Felix was waiting for us there, having driven up separately so he could leave after talking to Star. I didn't know how long Pepe and I would have to stay to investigate.

Felix had made better time than I did, probably because Pepe wanted me to stop twice, once for a bathroom break and once to get him some beef jerky at a convenience store. It had been raining in Seattle, but as we came over the pass, the rain disappeared. The sky was blue overhead and the air had the spicy smell of warm pine needles.

"I will check with her," Kale said. He walked a little bit away from us and pulled out a walkie-talkie. I heard the squawk as he turned it on and carried on a brief conversation.

I took advantage of his preoccupation to give Felix a quick hug. Pepe took advantage of the guard's preoccupation to go darting down the path.

"Hey! Come back!" I yelled after him. The guard looked up but didn't seem concerned. Little did he know Pepe. "Pepe! Come back!"

I looked at Felix, who said nothing, but I caught the twinkle in his eye, the twinkle that said *If you had only let me train your dog properly, he would come when you called.*

"Can I go get my dog?" I asked Kale. Pepe had vanished behind a curve in the path between the tall pines.

"Just a second . . ." I heard more squawking and then he looked up.

"Yes, you have permission to enter. Star wants to meet this Wolf Whisperer. She's in her inner sanctum at the main lodge."

We hurried down the path, trying to catch up with Pepe, but he had vanished from sight. The dirt path wound through the trees, until it came out on a rise, overlooking the cleared area that contained the buildings. We paused a minute to take in the idyllic scene. But there was no sign of Pepe.

"Where could he have gone?" I asked.

"Knowing Pepe, I would guess he is eating," said Felix. It's always a bit embarrassing when someone else knows your dog better than you do.

Because that's exactly where he was. In the dining hall at the lodge and sitting in the lap of my sister, Terry, who was feeding him bacon.

"Look, Geri!" Pepe said as we approached. "I found your sister."

"You got out!" I said, leaning over and giving Terry a big hug. "How did you manage that?"

She smiled but it seemed halfhearted. "Star got everything straightened out," she said.

"So you're not under arrest?"

She shook her head, but I could tell she was holding something back.

I introduced her to Felix.

"Wow!" he said, looking from one of us to the other. "You two look so alike! You could almost be twins."

"Really?" I was surprised. Terry had always been the acknowledged beauty of our family. We have the same dark, curly hair, but Terry has those killer green eyes, while mine are simply brown, and she also has a longer, leaner frame than me. Or maybe that was the result of good, clean living at the Dogawanda Center. Maybe I should give the Paleolithic diet a try.

"So this is the famous Wolf Whisperer," Terry said. "I understand Crystal has summoned you to her inner sanctum. That's a rare privilege. No outsider had ever entered it before. Here, I'll show you the way."

She unfolded herself from her chair and set Pepe down. She led us up the grand stairway in the center hall of the lodge, which split in two as it proceeded to the second floor, while the central portion remained open to the room below. We passed a door, which Terry said led to the administrative offices.

An elevator took us up another floor to a foyer, decorated rather incongruously, I thought, considering the rustic interior of the lodge, with a crystal chandelier and marble tiles and a huge gilt-covered door. Terry rang the bell and we heard a voice commanding us to enter. Terry gave me a quick hug before heading back down.

We stepped into an Arabian fantasy: Persian rugs, gold silk drapes, tall brass jars full of peacock feathers, low divans covered with pillows in shades of hot orange, pink, and mustard. A huge beam ran down the middle of the peaked roof and a chain of brass lanterns containing flickering candles hung from its length. The room smelled of jasmine and incense.

Star was lying on a divan in the middle of the room, propped up on gold pillows. She was wearing a pink silk caftan and lifted her arm languidly, beckoning for us to approach. Pepe sneezed.

"Ah, Towering Cedar!" said Star. "What fortuitous timing!"

"Towering Cedar?" Felix was confused.

"That's Pepe's Dogawandan name," I told him.

"I have the most amazing news to share with you," Star went on, holding out her arms to Towering Cedar, who jumped up on the divan, where he was immediately showered with kisses. I saw the marks her pink lipstick left on his white fur.

"What?" I asked.

"Let me show you," Star said. "Bring me my tape machine." She pointed to a small machine on a table near the door.

"Is it *musica*?" asked Pepe. "I can dance, you know," he told Star.

I fetched the tape recorder and brought it over to her.

"Take a seat," Star said to us.

The only places to sit were pillows on the floor beneath her thronelike chair.

"I hope she does not expect me to sing," said Pepe. "I once had a disastrous experience at *Teatro alla Scala*. The orchestra was—"

"I record each one of my channeling sessions," Star said. "It is the only way I can hear the wisdom of Dogawanda. He comes through me and my voice becomes his and I am always blank after the experience."

"I am that way often when I first wake up," said Pepe.

She turned the recorder on. As it started to play, we could hear Star's girlish voice announcing the arrival of Dogawanda, and then the gruff tones of the spirit himself, delivering his wisdom.

"Here!" said Star. "Listen carefully! There is another voice that overlaps Dogawanda's voice here. It is most perplexing."

She was right. I heard her voice speaking as Dogawanda, but I also heard Pepe's voice saying, "I am not a road. I am a Chihuahua."

"Did you hear the other voice?" Star asked me.

"It was me, of course," Pepe said.

"I'm not sure," I said. My thoughts were swirling. This was not the time or place to let Felix know that my dog talked. Plus, this seemed to imply that Star could hear him. Which bothered me for some reason.

"Listen!" said Star. The tape went on a little longer.

I heard Pepe say: "See, Geri, I told you I can bring you many riches."

"Did you hear that? The promise of treasure!" Star said.

"Geri!" said Pepe. He sounded thrilled. "I think she can hear me!"

"Of course, it is puzzling," said Star. "Not exactly what one expects from an entity, but . . ."

"What do you mean, entity?" I asked.

"Well, clearly this is another spirit coming through your dog," Star said. She turned to bow to him. "Or I should say Towering Cedar."

"Ah, I see!" I said.

"Why should she not believe that wisdom comes directly from a dog?" Pepe asked. "Why must she always credit a spirit?"

Yes, and I wondered why couldn't she hear him speaking in the room. She merely patted him on the head and said, "He's so adorable."

"So it's very important that you and Towering Cedar remain with us after the introductory weekend," Star went on.

"Yes, we would love to," I said. It would be the perfect cover for our investigation.

Crystal nodded. "I think you will progress rapidly through the levels. Artichoke will handle the oh-so-necessary but boring paperwork and payment arrangements. Meanwhile, I have been neglecting your guest."

Chapter 20

"You must be the famous Wolf Whisperer," said Star, turning her attention to Felix. I didn't like the way she looked at him, like she was hungry and he was good to eat. But he did look good. He was wearing a pair of slightly worn black jeans that fit really well, a black T-shirt, and a pair of well-worn cowboy boots. "How did you earn that title?"

Felix looked at me. I think he was asking for help. All I could do was shrug my shoulders.

"I grew up in L.A. My parents worked in the film industry and so do my siblings. I was always the one bringing home stray animals, and so it seemed logical for me to get involved in training animal actors. I've worked with wolves, big cats, and even"—he looked at Pepe—"Chihuahuas. I have to say that Chihuahuas are the most difficult animal to train of any I have yet encountered."

"That is because we are smarter than humans," said Pepe.

Star laughed. She had a girlish laugh, soft and light. "More difficult than wolves?"

Felix nodded. "Right now I'm working on a film being shot here in the Northwest that features wolves. However, we are still looking for the right animals."

"I understand you're interested in my wolf-dogs?" She said that in a soft and seductive voice.

"I am," said Felix. "How did you acquire them?"

"They were a gift," said Star, holding out her hand so Felix could help her to her feet, "from an admirer." She laughed again. "Would you like to see them?"

"Of course," said Felix.

"Are they still talking about wolves?" Pepe asked.

As we proceeded down the path through the woods to the pen, Star kept Felix beside her. But Pepe and I stayed close enough behind them to hear Star explaining how the principles the Doga-wandans learned from dog behavior created success and harmony for humans. Felix nodded now and then and politely uttered, "Oh, I see" and "That's interesting" and "Yes, dogs do have much to teach us."

"I have been telling you that for a long time, Geri," said Pepe.

"Yes, I know," I told him. (And it was true—I had learned a lot from my dog. I just didn't want it to go to his head.)

When we arrived outside the pen, the wolf-dogs were pacing back and forth.

"I think they heard us coming," said Pepe.

"They can sense us coming," Felix told Star. "They use all of their senses, not just hearing, but also scent."

"And what do *you* sense?" Star asked Felix.

He answered by giving me a sly wink, then opened the gate and calmly walked inside the enclosure with the two wolf-dogs.

Star gasped.

I closed my eyes.

When I opened them again, Felix was still alive and in one piece. In fact, the wolf-dogs were circling his legs. I held my breath, afraid to say a word for fear that it might cause the wolf-dogs to attack. A wolf could crush the bones of an elk in one mighty bite. Star was of the same mind, I think, because she was so frozen in place and ashen-faced that she could have been mistaken for a statue.

Pepe, on the other hand, muttered, "Show-off."

"Good wolves," said Felix, his tone low and even. "You are beautiful, lovely creatures."

"They are primitive beasts," said Pepe, "although they are my distant cousins."

"I'm just here to visit with you," Felix told the wolf-dogs, his tone reassuring. Then he did the inexplicable: He slowly sank into a squat, looking at each wolf-dog in turn. I had heard that you were never supposed to stare directly at a dog, particularly one that looked ready to attack. What was he thinking?

My heart was doing jumping jacks in my chest. Then one wolf-dog began to lick Felix's hand, the way Pepe sometimes licks me. The other wolf-dog lay down in front of Felix, forepaws extended, and gazed up at him, almost worshipfully.

Star gasped again. Then a smile spread slowly across her face.

Felix slowly stood up.

So did the wolf-dogs.

"Sit!" he said. There was a moment of hesitation, and then the giant beasts slowly lowered their rumps to the ground.

"They behave better than you," I said to Pepe.

"Sitting on command is just a parlor trick," said Pepe.

"Lie down," commanded Felix, putting out his hand, palm forward and lowering it toward the ground. The wolf-dogs bent their paws and lowered their heads and were soon stretched out in front of him.

"Nice work!" Felix said, giving each of them a quick rubdown, a scratch around the ears, a knuckle working down their backs. One of the animals rolled over and presented her snowy belly. I considered trying the same move myself once Felix left the pen.

Which he did, a few minutes later.

I let out a huge sigh of relief.

Star's smile grew even wider. "Remarkable," she

said. "That was utterly amazing," she told him. "You are truly dominant, Wolf Whisperer."

"I can work with these hybrids," said Felix. "It's obvious someone put some effort into training them. Do you know much about their background?"

Star shook her head.

"I could question them," Pepe said. He seemed a little put out that we were paying more attention to the wolf-dogs than to him. "Their language skills are basic compared to mine, but I should be able to translate."

"You really don't have the proper setup for them," Felix said. "They need exercise and training every day. And the pen is far too small. They require an area at least five times this size, especially if they are going to be cooped up for most of the day."

"We'll see what we can do," said Star. We began walking back toward the lodge. "When do you need them?"

"The sooner the better," said Felix. "We are looking for a new location for the outdoor scenes. Our film crew is in Seattle just waiting for the go-ahead."

"I can act," said Pepe. "I was once a stunt double for the most famous Chihuahua to ever appear in a Hollywood movie."

"What type of location are you looking for?" Star asked.

"An open meadow that is framed by big trees." Felix waved his hand at the pines and cedars that surrounded us. "We had a permit to shoot in a Seattle park, but it didn't work out."

"Because they banned the wolves?"

"No, it was just a schedule conflict. We started shooting too late and another group was planning an event at the same park."

"You can film in the meadow at the other end of the property," said Star. "You'd have a clear space for the wolves to run and a backdrop of trees." We had reached the edge of the woods, and Star paused, her hand on Felix's arm, pointing to the expanse of meadow behind the yurt.

"I also filled in for the most celebrated Chihuahua to ever advertise Mexican food," said Pepe.

"That would be ideal," Felix answered. "Especially the eastern exposure. We're hoping to shoot under the full moon on Monday night. But I would be concerned about working with these animals in an area that is so exposed. They will be under my control, but . . ."

"Don't worry!" said Star. "The property is completely fenced. And our fences are topped with razor wire."

"That's quite impressive," Felix said. "What are you trying to keep in?"

"Not in, but out," Star laughed. "You wouldn't believe how many people have tried to sneak into our grounds. Reporters hoping to get an inside scoop. Deprogrammers plotting to kidnap one of our devoted followers. Private investigators trying to get a message through to someone who has chosen to break off contact with their old pack."

Was it just my guilty conscience or was Star

looking straight at me when she said that? I tried to distract her by stepping forward and giving Felix a big hug.

"I'm just so glad you're safe," I said. "I was worried about you when you stepped inside that pen with the wolves."

"I'm worried about you, too," he whispered in my ear. "I wish I could be sure that you were safe." Out loud he said, "Don't worry about me. I'm a professional."

"So are we," said Pepe.

Chapter 21

"When do you want to begin?" Star asked as we headed up the steps toward the lodge.

"I'd like to spend the day with them tomorrow," Felix said. "Just to be sure they'll respond to my commands. If everything goes well, we could begin filming on Monday afternoon."

"Will you give our wolves credit in your film?" Star asked.

"Of course. However you like."

"Just a mention that they came from the Doga-wanda Center for Enlightenment," said Star.

"Sure. It never hurts to advertise."

Star smiled. "There are many ways to spread the Word of Dogawanda." She paused as we approached the front steps of the lodge. "In fact, I hope you will join us for the final session of our introductory seminar, which will begin in about an hour. You will be able to see our training principles in action."

"Well . . . ," Felix said.

I tried to jump in to help him out. "Perhaps Felix has to get back to—"

Star cut me off. "Your friend, Geri, or rather I should say her talented dog, Towering Cedar, will be the focal point of this ceremony."

"It is *bueno* to be recognized," said Pepe. "But I wonder what I am being recognized for?"

"What do you mean?" I asked.

"I will be channeling this new spirit who comes through him," she said. "It seems to be a feminine spirit. I wonder what we should call her?"

"Perhaps Wanda the Dog!" said Pepe.

"Perhaps Wanda," said Star dreamily as she drifted up the steps. "Excuse me, I must prepare myself."

"What is going on?" I said to my dog as Star left.

"What do you mean?" said Felix. "It seems pretty clear. The woman is *loco*."

"You didn't seem to think that when she was talking to you earlier," I said.

"Geri, I was being polite," Felix said. "Besides, I wanted to understand better what you are dealing with here. She definitely has some weird notions about dogs and their behavior."

"All of her ideas come from Dogawanda," I said.

"Come on, Geri," Felix said. "There is no Dogawanda. She's just making this stuff up."

"I don't know about that," I protested. "She seems to hear something." It seemed to be my dog. "And look at all these people." I waved my hand at the green-clad Dogawandans. Every one of them was smiling. "Would they be here if they weren't happy?"

"I wonder about that," said Felix. "Perhaps the fence is to keep people in, not to keep people out."

I pondered that. "I don't think so. The Dogawandans seemed able to get down to town when the sheriff wanted to talk to them."

Felix shrugged. "There are other ways to keep people confined," he said.

"What do you mean?"

"Psychological control. Suggesting that everything that happens outside is dangerous. She seems to rule by fear more than by positive reinforcement."

"You keep confusing having a relationship with a person with training a dog," I said. "They're totally different!"

"I certainly don't think I'm training you very well," said Felix. "If I were, we wouldn't be here right now. We'd be in bed and you would be training me in how to give you pleasure." He drew me into his arms and started to whisper into my ear suggestions about what I might like him to do to me.

"Geri!" said Pepe.

"Just a minute," I said to him. I wanted to hear more of Felix's ideas about how he would train me.

"Geri!" said Pepe again.

"Can't you see I'm busy?" I snapped.

"That's obvious," said a deep, sexy voice. I recognized that voice. It was the voice of Fox Black.

I pushed Felix away, a bit embarrassed, as if we had been caught doing the things Felix was suggesting. I could feel my face flush with warmth.

Fox Black was standing a few feet away, his head cocked to one side. He wore ripped black jeans and a tight black tank top. "Who's your new friend?" he asked.

"No friend of yours," said Pepe.

"Hey!" I chided him, then realized Fox probably thought I was talking to him.

"This is Felix," I said sternly. "He's a Wolf Whisperer."

Felix looked mortified.

"What's a Wolf Whisperer?" Fox asked in a tone that was full of derision. Was he feeling some animosity toward Felix?

"I work with wild animals," said Felix. "I tame them." His dark eyes seemed especially piercing. His head was thrust out a little.

"I recognize the posture of male animals vying for dominance," said Pepe.

"Why, Pepe!" I said. "You have an excellent grasp of body language. I do believe you could train humans."

"Of course," said Pepe. "All dogs train humans."

"Of course," said Felix. "It's part of my training."

"Of course," said Fox. "It's part of the training program."

Apparently, Fox thought I meant him and Felix thought I was referring to him. They continued to face each other, fists clenched, bodies leaning forward.

I wanted to break up the tension. "At what level do you learn that?" I asked.

Fox broke off his gaze with Felix. I saw Felix toss his head back a little, as if to announce his victory in the eye-staring contest.

"Humans are so obvious," said Pepe.

Fox turned to me. "At the beta level, we study body language extensively. I understand that you're moving up to that level."

"Yes, I am," I said, casting a sideways glance at Felix, who crossed his arms.

"Star asked me to take you to the office so you could register. After the graduation ceremony, you'll be moving to the beta den," he said. "You and your little dog."

"Tell him I'm not a little dog!" said Pepe.

"He's not a little dog," I said. "His name is Towering Cedar."

"Well, then you and Towering Cedar." He held out his elbow and I looked back at Felix.

"However, the beta pack headquarters is off-limits to anyone who has not completed the introductory training," said Fox, looking at Felix.

"It's OK," I told Felix. "It will only take me a few minutes to register. Will you meet me in the dining room? It would be great if you could stay for the evening session."

Felix merely shrugged.

Chapter 22

"Geri, this is very good," said Towering Cedar as we sat on a bench in the hall on the second floor of the lodge, waiting to meet Artichoke. It sounded like she was arguing with someone inside her office, but I couldn't hear the other person's voice. "We will soon be part of the beta pack, plus you have two males both trying to mark you as their territory," Pepe went on.

"That's not exactly how I think about it," I said, though I had to admit I was really surprised by the unexpected attention from Fox Black. The fact that he had dialed it down a lot after we left Felix's presence was disappointing, but since I assumed flirting was just part of his nature, I didn't take it too seriously.

"Well, you can be sure that Felix is even more interested in you now," said Pepe. "I could smell it on him!"

"Are you sure?" I asked. "He looked sort of annoyed. I wouldn't be surprised if he left."

"Oh no, he will stay around to claim his prize," said Pepe. "Trust me!"

Just then, the door opened and Artichoke appeared. She wore a dark green velvet vest over a long, tiered green skirt.

"Ah, Crystal told me you would be continuing with us," she said. "Come in!"

"How are you doing?" I asked as she waved me to a seat across from her desk. She did not seem like the distraught woman we had last seen. Her hair was braided and coiled in a tight bun on her head.

"I am in the Now," she said, as if she did not know what I meant.

"I mean, after finding the body," I said, leaning forward.

Artichoke pondered that for a minute. "Everyone passes away," she said. "For Leaf, that time was yesterday. But she is now with Dogawanda on the other side. That is not cause for dismay or grief as it would be for those who are unevolved."

OK. That put me in my place. Artichoke turned to look at her computer screen. I saw there was also a telephone on her desk.

"Oh, so you do have Internet and phones here," I said.

"Yes, but I am the only one who has access. For others, it would be a distraction. It would take them out of the Now."

Artichoke pushed some papers across the desk

toward me. "This is our standard contract. If you will just sign here and there"—she pointed to some lines at the end of the three-page document—"and give me your credit card, I can get you out of here in time to have dinner before the evening session."

"I'd love to read this," I said, peering at the page of text, which was set in a tiny font.

"It just indemnifies us from any legal claim that might result if you were injured in any way by the training or some mishap that happened while you were staying with us," Artichoke explained. "It also prevents you from disclosing anything you learn about while on our premises."

"Has that happened?" I asked.

"Well, sometimes people leave. Sometimes we find they are not suitable candidates for Dogawanda's wisdom. They may have some bad feelings as a result and sometimes they express their dissatisfaction publicly. Or someone thinks they can go off and create their own school, using Dogawanda's wisdom. This document makes it clear that we will sue if either of those things happens."

"You would think that Dogawanda would appreciate others spreading the word," I said, my pen poised over the signature line.

Artichoke was not amused. "It's important that the principles are presented in the right context. They can be easily misconstrued."

"I do not agree to these terms, Geri," said Pepe. "But as long as you are signing and not me, we should be OK."

Artichoke took my credit card and wrote down the numbers. She had another form I had to sign to give my permission for the charge. Five thousand dollars for one week of beta-level classes. I hoped that Jimmy G would be able to recoup the cost from Mark.

"That is a lot of money, Geri," said Pepe.

"How many others are continuing on?" I asked Artichoke.

"We'll see after the dinner," she replied. "That's where we make the formal pitch. And sometimes candidates decide after the graduation ceremony. It's very powerful."

"So how come we got signed up early?" I asked.

"You're very lucky," Artichoke said, standing up to indicate our session was over. "Crystal has taken a special interest in your little dog. I understand he has a role to play in the graduation ceremony."

"I am not a little dog," Pepe said.

"He is not a little dog," I said.

"He most certainly is," said Artichoke firmly.

"It sounds like you don't approve of him," I said. I felt like I should defend my dog.

"Whatever Dogawanda wants is what I want," Artichoke said crisply. "I'm just not convinced that Dogawanda would ever choose to speak through a Chihuahua."

Chapter 23

I didn't get much of a chance to talk with Felix over dinner. We were assigned tables; the idea seemed to be to pair up someone who had come for the introductory weekend with a beta-level and an alpha-level Dogawandan. If it was anything like our table, the goal was to persuade the prospect to sign up for the next level by talking about the benefits and wisdom to come. I saw checkbooks being handed over at other tables and credit cards as well.

Felix did not seem to be enjoying his dinner at all. In fact, he seemed to be arguing with the Dogawandans at his table, but I didn't get a chance to talk to him again because Pepe and I were whisked away to the Longhouse to prepare for the final ceremony.

But Pepe was right; when Star ushered us out onto the stage set up at the front of the Longhouse, I saw Felix leaning against the wall in the back of the room. He was half in shadow, so I couldn't really read the expression on his face.

Star took her usual place, sitting on a chair in the center of the stage. She had placed another chair beside her, full of pillows, and Pepe was posed on top of the pile, which made him almost as tall as Star. He had adopted a Sphinx-like pose, lying down, facing the audience with his paws in front of him.

I was supposed to sit facing the audience, at the left-hand side of the stage, where I had to crane my head at an awkward angle to see Pepe, but he insisted I remain close at hand. Fox Black was seated on the other side of the stage, and I could feel his eyes on me. I tried to ignore him since I didn't want to give Felix the wrong impression.

The entire Longhouse was filled. The Dogawandans in the inner circle, like Terry and Artichoke, were sitting on pillows in the middle of the room, and the participants were lined up on the benches. Felix was all the way at the back.

"Greetings, loved ones," said Star. She was wearing a cloud-white garment that shimmered in the light of the candles that were arrayed in glass jars at the front of the stage. A single floor lamp illuminated her teased blond hair and Pepe's white fur, so they seemed to glow in the darkness. "You are in for a fabulous treat tonight, something that will be talked about around the world tomorrow."

A whisper, a sigh, a gasp rippled through the crowd.

"Yes, after many years of channeling Doga-wanda," Star said, "I have the extraordinary privilege of introducing you to a new entity, an entity that I am able to channel because of this amazing being." She waved her hand at Pepe and he sat up and took a bow.

There was a faint ripple of laughter in the crowd.

"He may look small," she said, "but his soul contains dimensions." She folded her hands in her lap and bowed her head. She seemed to be falling asleep, and I didn't blame her. It was dark and warm in the Longhouse and the air was thick with the scent of beeswax and incense.

"When do I get to talk?" asked Pepe.

"Hush!" I said, motioning for him to be quiet.

Star's head snapped up. In the gloom, her face seemed to elongate. Her golden eyes seemed to glow in the darkness. Her voice was gruff, almost like a bark.

"Dogawanda greets his servants," she said.

"I didn't say anything," said Pepe.

Star seemed startled. She turned to look at Pepe, shook her head, then bowed it again. Nothing happened for many minutes, but everyone in the room remained perfectly still. When Pepe spoke again, I was sure everyone could hear him.

He said, "Greetings, followers of Towering Cedar."

Star shivered slightly. Then she lifted her head,

and this time her voice was lighter, more lilting than it had been when she channeled Dogawanda.

"Towering Cedar welcomes you!"

The crowd gasped as one.

"Yes," Star went on smoothly, "I am a new entity coming to you through the channel of this Chihuahua." She turned to bow to Pepe, who blinked. He always looks particularly wise when he blinks, although that usually happens right before he falls asleep. "And through my beloved vessel, Crystal Star."

"So she can hear me, Geri!" said Pepe, looking at me.

"Yes, I can hear the words of this entity known as Towering Cedar as they form in the mind of this mighty creature," Star declared, her voice growing in volume.

Pepe seemed to be waking up. "This is *magnifico*!" he declared.

"It is magnificent," said Star, "as you are all my beloved followers."

"I wonder if they will do as I tell them?" Pepe mused.

"Dear ones, I call you to follow my precepts. You must live in alignment with the divine order of the Dog," Star said.

"Towering Cedar commands you . . . ," Pepe began.

"And Towering Cedar commands you . . ." Star paused.

"You must all bark!" said Pepe.

"To bark?" Star looked at Pepe.

"*Sí*, bark like a dog!" said Pepe.

"To bark," Star commanded, "and so align with the dog within."

Immediately the room erupted in a cacophony of yips and yowls, ruffs and roars. Everyone seemed to have a different interpretation of what a bark sounded like. The only person I could see who seemed unmoved was Felix, who had his arms folded and his mouth firmly shut. I pretended to bark while turning to Pepe and glaring at him.

Star waved her arms and the din subsided. "Towering Cedar advises you to bark for at least ten minutes a day," she said. "First thing in the morning. It will help you release negative feelings and the demons of insecurity."

"I said no such thing," said Pepe. "I just wanted to see if they would obey."

"Towering Cedar is well pleased," said Star, "and thanks you for your obedience. As you know, obedience to the alpha is an important tenet of the Dogawandan code. In fact, it is the second commandment of Dogawanda."

"And the first commandment of Towering Cedar is this," said Pepe. "Beware of those who try to train you. They desire to control you. Never trust them!"

"Indeed, Towering Cedar affirms that you must trust those who train you."

"That is not what I said," declared Pepe. "That is the opposite of what I said."

"It is called a paradox," said Star, "for through perfect obedience comes perfect freedom."

"Wait a minute!" said Pepe.

"And now we will conclude by reciting the Seven Commandments of Dogawanda," said Star.

"But only after I tell the story of my life as a temple dog in the service of the moon goddess, Coyolxauhqui." I could see that my dog did not want to give up the limelight and was making things up as usual.

"But first," said Star, "I will reveal myself to you as the Aztec moon goddess, Ixoli-Pixoli."

"No way, Jose!" said Pepe, sounding annoyed. "I said temple dog." Then after a pause. "OK, but if you want the moon goddess"—his voice rose an octave—"I will give you the moon goddess." He sat up straighter. "I saw the great unhappiness of my people and decided to descend to earth in the form of a little white dog. A brave dog. A noble dog. A dog who would lead his people to great victories."

"I am here to lead you to great victories," Star said. "I take this humble form to inspire you so that you know that even if we seem small, we can achieve greatness. Look within and you will find the courage to continue on the path of Dogawanda."

"And now you must worship me," said Pepe. "I accept cash, checks, and credit cards."

"The moon goddess requests you show your respect by showering this gentle creature that does her bidding with affection," Star said. "And now I bid you adieu!" She slumped in her chair, and Fox

Black hurried to her side. He seemed worried about her. They held a whispered consultation. She kept shaking her head and glancing at Pepe. Then she stood up.

"I hope you are well satisfied," she told the crowd. "Fox tells me that you got to meet the new entity I was privileged to channel for you." There was a murmur of appreciation from the crowd. "This is a watershed moment for us," Star said. "It means that we will be able to expand our programs and include the wisdom of the Aztec empire along with the wisdom of the Dog. I will be announcing a new level of training in the next week. For now, I hope that you will join me in a howl of praise and mystery."

After the howl and the formal acceptance of the graduates into the community, which was achieved by making a circle around them through which they had to pass, we all filed out into the evening air. It was starting to get cold. A few stars were visible over the tops of the trees and the sky was filled with orange and pink clouds in the west.

Pepe was in the center of a swarm of acolytes who wanted to touch him. I think he was disappointed they weren't offering money, but he settled for petting.

"Wasn't that amazing?" I said to Felix.

"What?" said Felix. "That your dog barked and Star pretended he was speaking?"

"That's all you heard? Pepe barking?"

"And Star making up ridiculous stories." He looked at me with troubled eyes. "What am I missing here?"

I tried to act casual. "Nothing. It's just that sometimes I feel like I can hear Pepe talking."

"Dogs are very expressive, that's true," Felix said. "And they communicate with us in many subtle ways, that's true. But dogs don't talk and dogs don't channel Aztec goddesses. Leave it to humans to come up with such bizarre concepts. The wonder is that she can make money off this nonsense."

"And so will we, Geri!" said Pepe, bounding over to us. "I think I'm getting the hang of this channeling scam."

Chapter 24

The initiates began leaving, calling good-byes, which echoed in the evening air. Dusk was falling and people wanted to get off the mountain before it became dark. They were returning to their regular lives and real jobs, while Pepe and I were staying behind. Felix wanted me to leave—he said he was worried that I was getting in too deep—but I told him I had a job to do.

As I wandered back to my lodgings, I was annoyed with Felix for not trusting me and feeling lonely because he left without me. So when Fox Black popped up on the path, I was happy to see him.

"Great show your dog put on!" he said.

"*Gracias*," said Pepe.

"Yes, he's quite talented," I said. "And he's got quite an ego as well."

"That goes along with the territory," said Fox.

"Territory?" asked Pepe. "Is he talking about marking territory? I do that, too!"

"What do you mean?" I asked.

"Those who have a big talent need a big ego to handle their responsibilities," said Fox.

"Oh!" I hadn't thought of that. My dog was pretty talented for a dog.

"What are you doing now?" Fox asked.

"I think I'm supposed to meet my alpha," I said, "and move my stuff to the Beta Barn."

"How about joining me at the hot springs for a glass of champagne afterward?" Fox asked. "To celebrate your graduation."

"That sounds lovely!" I said. "I could use a nice relaxing soak."

"You could use a new boyfriend," said Pepe.

"Great, I'll see you there in ten minutes," said Fox with a wink.

I was a little surprised to learn that my alpha was Artichoke, since she had never seemed to like me. But maybe that was what made her the ideal alpha. She was waiting in my room when I got back to the Bunkhouse and she seemed impatient.

She stood there with her arms crossed, watching as I stuffed my clothes into my suitcase. Pepe tried to help by bringing over a few nibbles of food and tucking them into various corners.

"Artichoke is such an interesting name," I said,

thinking a compliment might soften her up. "How did you get it?"

"Dogawanda gave it to me," said Artichoke. "He said I was all prickles on the outside and a soft heart within."

"I suppose that's a good thing," I observed.

"Not for you," said Artichoke. "You will see only my prickles. My job is to teach you to obey without thinking. Only then will you be relieved of the worries that plague humans. And right now I say that you should make it snappy. I don't have all day to stand around chatting about names."

I tried not to take it personally.

"When do I get my name?" I asked as we headed across the compound, me dragging my bright blue rolling suitcase. Pepe trotted beside me, stopping to sniff and water various patches of the lawn.

"When you have earned it," Artichoke said.

We stopped outside the whitewashed barn. "This is the Beta Barn, your new home." Artichoke opened one of the doors and we were inside a gloomy hallway, with doors on either side, stretching into the distance. "These were once the stalls," said Artichoke. "We cleaned them out and made them into bedrooms."

Halfway down the hall, Artichoke stopped outside a door. I had noticed that each door had a placard with a name on it: CLOUD, LILY, SEED, QUAIL. The placard on the door we were facing read LEAF. Artichoke frowned at it and tore it off.

"Someone was supposed to be sure the room was clean for you," she said.

"This was where Leaf lived?" I asked. My voice quivered a little.

"Yes," said Artichoke. She had thrown open the door and gone inside. The room was tiny, just barely big enough for a single bed with an iron frame. A small window above the bed was too high to provide a view or any ventilation.

"It looks clean," Artichoke said, backing out of the room so I could step inside.

"Maybe we will find a clue within," said Pepe, running in after me and darting under the bed.

"Where am I supposed to put my suitcase?" I asked. It was still out in the hall.

"We have a storage room at the end of the hall. You won't need any of these things you brought. We are free from materialistic concerns. We have two changes of clothing. When one gets dirty, we put it in the laundry chute and wear the other. You should have been issued a uniform. I don't know why that hasn't happened yet." Artichoke frowned again.

"What happened to all of the things that belonged to Leaf?" I asked.

"I don't know," said Artichoke. "I assume the police took them." She headed off down the hall. "I'll show you where the storage locker is."

"Did you find anything?" I asked Pepe.

"I think so," said Pepe. "I will show you when we go back."

"No, we didn't find anything that would explain why she would leave. She seemed to have adjusted well." Artichoke thought I was talking to her.

"What makes you think she was leaving?" I asked. I was still haunted by the idea that Tammy's death was my fault.

This was the first time I actually saw a reaction from Artichoke. She stopped in her tracks. "Well, she was outside the property, wasn't she? Betas just don't go outside the property. Not without permission and not without a dog walker."

"Dog walker?"

"That's what we call them. Perhaps it would be more accurate to say a chaperone. We just want to protect them from the negativity in the outside world. It's a critical stage in their development. Betas can easily be spoiled by too much discipline or too little."

I hated the way she kept on talking about people as if they were dogs. But then I wondered how dogs felt about the way we talked about them. Or maybe the way Felix talked about Pepe. I should let Felix know that Pepe could talk. That would clear up so many things in our relationship.

Artichoke continued down the hall, stopping to point out the communal bathrooms at the back of the barn, one on one side for the women and one on the other side for the men. The storage unit was against the back wall, under the staircase. It was full of dusty suitcases and duffel bags and knapsacks, and it was unlocked.

A flight of stairs led up to a large open area, what had once been the hayloft. It had been carpeted with green shag and furnished with many pillows, in various shades of green and brown. The room was full of Dogawandans, all in their regulation light green cotton skirts and pants, vests, and tunic tops. Some were sitting cross-legged, apparently meditating, and others were gathered in small groups talking.

"We encourage all the betas to spend most of their time here," said Artichoke. "It's important for you to establish your place in the pack." She pointed to a whiteboard hung along one wall. "Of course, when you start out, we give you the most submissive position." Various chores were written in felt-tip pen, apparently in the order of their preference, and in the grids next to them were written the names of the various members of the beta pack. I recognized some from the doors downstairs.

Artichoke studied the chart and then rubbed out Leaf's name. She was listed as a food server. She bumped up the people on the chart below Leaf, so Seed was now a food server, and wrote me in at the bottom of the chart under "rock mover."

"What does a rock mover do?" I asked.

"It means you find rocks and bring them to the rock-cleaning station," Artichoke said. "We need many rocks for the walkways and terraces for the new structure. You'll be doing that every morning for two hours a day. Quail will show you how to do it. He's a rock mover, too."

"What about the other new betas?" I asked as she wrote in my name: Geri. I really wanted a cool Dogawandan name. Maybe I would be a flower like an iris (one of my favorites) or a cool animal, like an otter.

"Don't concern yourself with others," said Artichoke. "They will be assigned tasks that are appropriate for them. Now I'm going to leave you. You need to find your own place in the pack. You will report to me first thing in the morning. You can find me at the level four table in the dining hall." She turned and vanished down the stairs.

As soon as she left, several of the Dogawandans rushed over to us. They wanted to know more about the moon goddess, how I had found such a talented dog, how Crystal had learned of his amazing abilities.

"I knew he was special the first moment I saw him," I said, remembering the day I had gone to the shelter to adopt one of the many rescued Chihuahuas flown up to Seattle from Los Angeles and how Pepe had caught my eye. It wasn't until I got him home that I realized he could talk.

"So can you actually hear him?" asked someone else.

"Well, yes, he speaks to me all the time," I said, glad that I had finally found people who would believe that my dog talked, yet I was impatient to get out of there to meet Fox.

"You are so lucky!" sighed one woman.

"Yes, you are lucky!" said Pepe, who was having his tummy rubbed by another Dogawandan devotee.

"There! He just spoke!" I said. "Did you hear that?"

The person petting his stomach drew back. The woman who told me I was lucky raised her eyebrows. "He just barked," she said.

"Yes!" I said, pretending that was what I meant. "He's very talkative."

Chapter 25

The concrete path to the hot springs was lit by lanterns set low to the ground. It wound through the woods in back of the lodge and ended at a small clearing that had been paved with concrete as well and was circled by mighty pine trees. The steam from the hot springs shrouded the boulders that served as a backdrop. Lights set low to the ground illuminated the shape of the boulders and sparkled on the bubbling surface of the hot springs.

I laid my towel on the large boulder beside the main pool and prepared to take off the bathrobe that I'd also brought from my room. I hadn't thought to bring a swimsuit with me to the Dogawan-dan compound and was clad only in my black bra and matching black panties.

I wasn't sure about the etiquette of the hot springs and figured that in the darkness, anyone who saw me would assume I was wearing a black bikini, especially as I'd already be in the water, which was a milky white color and topped with a froth of foam.

I peeled off my robe and took a few steps into the steaming water. It was just a little over body temperature. The contrast with the cold of the night air brought out goose bumps on my skin. I plunged in to my shoulders. Wide, flat rocks had been placed as seats around the bottom of the pool. When I sat on one, the water bubbled right around my collarbone. I started to feel my tensions melt away almost immediately.

"Comfortable?" asked Pepe, nuzzling the back of my head with his muzzle.

I turned and gave him a pat. "Totally," I said. "Say, aren't you coming in?"

Pepe shuddered. "No way, Jose," he said. He claims he has been afraid of the water ever since he was tossed into the deep end of a swimming pool in Beverly Hills. He took a couple steps to the right and lay down on the rock next to me, his forepaws hanging over it just above the water. "For now, I am content just to breathe in these interesting smells rising in the steam from the pool. The scents of the minerals and the warmth are quite soothing."

"I'm glad you're comfortable," I told him, then turned back and enjoyed the way the various lights sparkled and danced across the water. It reminded me of the fairy tales I'd read as a child. Everything about the setting was just magical—so magical, that I expected a handsome prince to show up to take me away to live happily ever after.

And so he did.

In this case, the handsome prince was Fox Black.

He wore flip-flops and a deep green, short Japanese-style bathrobe and carried a bottle of champagne.

He smiled when he saw me—a brilliant white smile, quite apparent even though the night was half upon us. His pale skin contrasted sharply with his long, jet-black hair.

I smiled back. Even though half of me started to feel half guilty about accepting his invitation, the other half of me felt like screaming and giggling and jumping up and down with the same hysteria that young women always exhibited at his rock concerts. Unfortunately, my parents had never let me attend one, so I had only seen him perform on MTV.

"You beat me here," he said, walking around the pool toward me. "And you have Towering Cedar with you. Greetings, blessed dog."

"*Hola*, yourself," Pepe told him.

Fox stopped a few feet away, set down the bottle of champagne, and took off his robe. He was totally nude! I tried my best to look only into Fox's eyes as he kicked off his flip-flops and slid into the pool beside me, but I couldn't help but notice that his entire body was covered with tattoos and that he was definitely well endowed.

"Ah, that's better," Fox said, his bare hip brushing against mine as he sat down beside me. I shivered.

"Keep your hands above the water, mister," warned Pepe.

"What did you say, Towering Cedar?" asked Fox. "Or should I call you Moon Goddess?"

"You can call me *el jefe*," Pepe told him.

Fox nodded as if he'd understood my dog's remark, which of course he couldn't have, then turned his intensely dark eyes to me. "Like some champagne?" he asked.

Before I could respond, he picked up the bottle, pointed it away, and untwisted the wire that held the cork in place. *Pop!* It went flying into the nearby woods, and a froth of bubbles spilled out of the neck and into the hot springs, blending in with the froth already on the surface of the water. I giggled. I couldn't help it. This was a fantasy come true, sitting in the hot springs, with the stars overhead and the smell of the pine trees all around us.

Fox took a swig off the bottle and handed it to me. It was chilled. I followed his example and tried to take a delicate sip but got a little more than I expected. It ran down my chin. I felt so decadent. Fox leaned over and licked the extra champagne off my chin. I almost swooned.

"Hey," Pepe told me. "I am the only one who can lick you."

"Shhhh," I told him.

"What?" said Fox, drawing back.

"Oh," I told him. "I was, uh, just stifling a sneeze, that's all."

"Bless you, then," he said.

"Well thanks, Fox," I said.

He smiled.

I smiled.

There was an awkward silence. The mood had somehow changed. It was almost like a first date that had started to go south (except for the fact that I was clad only in my underwear while sitting beside a naked rock star).

"We should try and get some information from him," Pepe told me. "Since Senor Fox has been coming here for a long time, he may know something that could help our case."

"So, Fox," I said, "how long have you been coming here?"

"Almost ten years," he said thoughtfully, taking another swig of champagne before passing the bottle along to me.

"So you have been a Dogawandan for a long time?" I asked, taking another swig from the bottle. The bubbles fizzed through my brain.

"Yes, I attribute all of my success to Dogawanda. I was a nobody when I first met Crystal. It was Dogawanda's advice that got me to where I am today."

"Wow!" I said. "Like what kind of advice?" I handed back the champagne bottle.

"Dogawanda encouraged me to play the guitar instead of writing songs and singing. That was the turning point in my career."

"Oh! I didn't know you sang!" I said. He was famous for his guitar riffs.

"Yes, well, I'm getting back into that," he said.

"I'd love to hear you sing," I said.

Fox smiled. He had a wolfish face in the moonlight: a long snout and glittering golden eyes. "I'll write you a song," he said.

Wow! I almost swooned.

"It's nice to meet someone who isn't judging me. Or trying to put me in a box," he said. "Everybody thinks they know me. Nobody listens except for what they want to hear."

"I'm sorry to hear that, Fox."

"Nobody hears me either," said Pepe.

"I really appreciate your listening, Geri," Fox said, putting his arm around my bare shoulders. Pepe growled softly. "Your little dog is very protective," Fox said with a laugh.

"The moon goddess is not amused," said Pepe.

I felt the sudden urge to tell Fox about my talented dog. Maybe it was the wine talking. "I guess I am good at listening," I said. "For instance, I can hear my dog talking."

"That's amazing!" Fox said, putting his fingers under my chin and tipping it up. "I wish you could teach me how." He studied me, his eyes half closed, those big, luscious lips so close to mine. The moonlight poured down on us, and the warm water surged around our bodies. All thoughts of Pepe evaporated. Only he was talking.

"Geri!" said Pepe. "You are about to be interrupted."

I waved my hand at him, trying to shut him up. I didn't want to spoil the moment.

"I think you might want to back off!" said Pepe.

"Never mind," I said. "You were saying, Fox?"

"I was saying—" He moved his lips closer to mine. "What a surprise!"

I looked up. It was my sister. She was standing in the moonlight, just a few feet from the hot springs, completely nude.

Chapter 26

"Having a party, are we, Fox?" she asked as she stepped down into the hot springs. The steam enveloped her lithe body. Fox had moved away and taken his arm from my shoulders. He passed the champagne bottle to Terry.

"Why are you wearing your underwear, Geri?" she said, glancing over at me after taking a swig of champagne.

"I didn't bring a swimsuit," I said a bit defensively.

"No one wears swimsuits here," she said. "We like to soak au naturel."

"Has anyone ever told you that you two look alike?" Fox said, looking from one of us to the other. "You two could be sisters!"

"Oh, come on, Fox," said Terry. "You know we are."

"What? How does he know that?" I asked.

"Star told him," Terry said. "She has a dossier on everyone who comes up here."

"How do you think Dogawanda knows all the things he knows about people's lives?" asked Fox.

"You mean Star does some kind of background check on people?" I asked, still not believing what I was hearing.

"Not Star. Artichoke. She's the only one who has access to a computer."

"Did she do research on me before I came?" I asked Terry.

She shrugged. "I assume so."

"Then she must have learned about me," said Pepe. "Perhaps that is why she invited us."

I suddenly got a chill. Did Star know that I was working for Jimmy G? That would mean Artichoke would know that as well.

"Did she know we were sisters?" I asked Terry.

"No, she couldn't possibly have known that," said Terry. "She doesn't even know my real name." She took another swig of the champagne, then handed the bottle back to Fox. "Or at least she didn't." She seemed glum.

"Do you have a lot of money?" Fox asked me.

I looked at him, stricken.

"Actually, yes," I said, thinking of the rather large reward Pepe and I had received after our last case.

"So now you know why you're here!" said Fox, raising the champagne bottle in a toast to me. "Star has a certain type she likes and she likes them loaded."

"Doesn't that seem dishonest?" I asked.

"What?" asked Fox.

"What?" asked Terry.

"What?" asked Pepe.

"That she gathers information about people and then uses it to con them into believing in Dogawanda?"

"A little deception is good for the soul," said Fox. "We can't handle too much reality."

"So you believe the end justifies the means?" I asked.

"Yes!" said Fox. "If the end result is more money."

"What about murder?" I said. "Is murder ever justified?"

Terry looked at me in horror. "What do you mean, murder?"

"Tammy was murdered," I said.

Terry reared back like she had been punched. "What makes you think Leaf was murdered?"

"Just the way the police questioned me," I said, realizing quickly that to say anything else would betray my true motivation. Talk about a means to an end. My end was to discover who had killed Tammy. Even if it meant grilling my own sister.

"You do have an active imagination, Geri," said Terry. "She was killed by wild animals in the woods while she was trying to sneak away from the ranch. Isn't that obvious?"

"Not to me," I said.

"Poor Leaf!" said Fox.

Terry motioned for Fox to pass her the champagne bottle and took another sip. "So the sheriff thinks someone killed her?"

"That's what I heard."

"Well, that makes sense now," Terry said. "They just kept grilling me over and over again about that last conversation."

"What did you talk about?" I asked.

"Basically she was homesick. She wanted to leave," Terry said. "She was going to go home and get her dog. She said it wasn't fair that you could bring your dog and she had to leave hers behind. But she said she had to get her money back first."

"Did she get it?" I asked.

"I don't know," Terry said. "I told her she had to talk to Artichoke about that. She handles all of the bookkeeping. But we kept on talking and after a while, she calmed down. She agreed that she needed to do more work on herself. After that, I didn't see her."

There was a long silence. Fox looked strained.

"What?" Terry asked. "Did you see her?"

Fox looked abashed. "She showed up at the hot springs late that night after everyone else was gone."

"And what sort of mood was she in?"

"She was weepy," said Fox. "Unsure of what to do. I tried to console her."

"And how did that go?" Terry asked.

"She didn't want to be consoled," said Fox.

Terry was curious. "So you might have been the last person to see her alive?"

"I guess," said Fox. He looked very uncomfortable. He shifted around on the rock.

"I warned her about you!" Terry said.

"What about him?" I asked, looking from him to her.

"Oh, he always seduces the new women," Terry said.

Now it was my turn to shift around on the rock, moving away from Fox.

"You know Star has asked you not to mess with the betas," Terry said. "They're too vulnerable."

"Star uses me to lure them here," said Fox. "I don't know why she objects to rewarding me for my efforts."

I was beginning to resent being talked about like I was a dog treat. I waded across to another rock.

"So what happened to Leaf?" I asked.

Fox shrugged. "She was still here when I left. Crying. That was it."

"And she was alone?"

"Yes." He took back the champagne bottle and took another deep swig. "I feel totally guilty. Maybe she drowned herself out of despair."

He really thought a lot of himself if he thought a woman would kill herself because he rejected her.

"I thought she was killed by wild animals," said Terry.

"Maybe they came upon her body floating in the water and carried her off," Fox suggested.

"Did you hear anything that would make you suspect that?" I asked.

"I was a little bit preoccupied," Fox said with a big grin.

"What do you mean preoccupied?" I asked, then got a sinking feeling.

"Hey, what can a fox do when he meets a hen right in his path?" He spread out his hands wide. "And for your information"—he turned to Terry—"it wasn't one of the new women."

Chapter 27

"Who was it?" I asked.

"A gentleman doesn't tell," said Fox.

"As if you were a gentleman!" said Terry, giving him a playful jab in the ribs. She grabbed the champagne bottle out of his hands and took another sip. "Hey, it's empty!"

"I'll go get another one," said Fox. He lifted himself out of the water. His pale limbs flashed silver in the moonlight. I turned my head aside but not before I got a good view of his private parts.

"Not bad," observed Pepe, "but proportionally, a Chihuahua has the advantage."

"Hush!" I said.

Terry lay back in the pool, her head tilted up toward the night sky. She looked around at the tops of the trees, which stood like dark sentinels around us. She gave a deep sigh. "I'm going to miss all of this," she said.

I couldn't believe what I was hearing. "Are you coming home with me?" I was overjoyed.

"No, Geri!" She straightened up and looked at me. Her eyes glittered in the darkness. "You're the reason I have to leave."

"What are you talking about?"

"I guess I can tell you now," she said, "since you'll never see me again."

"What do you mean?"

"I was in the witness protection program, but then I left. It's a long story."

"I want to hear it!"

"Well, you remember I was dancing at a strip club?" she asked.

I nodded. That's why Cheryl had kicked her out of the house.

"Why was she protecting witnesses?" asked Pepe.

"I was dating one of the bouncers. And the club owner hired him to do a hit. My boyfriend killed the guy, but the police caught him. In exchange for a reduced sentence, he agreed to testify against his boss. It was a big takedown because his boss was the head of a crime family. The feds had been trying to make a case against him for years. They put me in the witness protection program because they thought I might be in danger."

"And you couldn't call me or Cheryl and let us know that?"

Terry winced. "I could have contacted you, but I was scared. Afraid that someone would make the connection between me and you guys. And then you'd be in danger. I figured it was safer if I just disappeared."

"So you're still in the witness protection program?" The Dogawanda Center seemed like a strange place to hide a witness.

"No, after my boyfriend got out of prison, things got a little weird. I had been to a Dogawanda seminar and realized the Center was the perfect place to hide. No contact with the outside world, a new name . . ." Her voice trailed off.

"So you weren't rich when you came here?"

Terry laughed. "Far from it. But I worked hard to make myself invaluable. And for a while, it all seemed wonderful. But the closer I got to Crystal, the more I realized she wasn't the perfect person I thought. Of course, it's Dogawanda who's perfect. I mean, humans are always frail."

"Yes, it is dogs who are perfect," Pepe agreed.

"But still, it's hard to respect someone who's so selfish and greedy."

"So you're going to leave because you're disillusioned?"

"Not just that," she said. "But once you told the police my real name, they tracked me back to the witness protection program. The marshalls came and talked to me. They offered me a chance to move again and start a new life. It might be my one chance to get out of here."

"What do you mean?" I asked.

Before she could answer, we heard the sound of voices on the path, and Fox came tripping back, carrying another two champagne bottles, with a naked woman on each arm.

I stood up, thinking it was time to leave. I felt a little foolish about my assumption that Fox would be interested in me. He was just flirting. It was part of his nature.

Pepe, to my surprise, didn't tell me "I told you so." He was eager to get back to our room in the Beta Barn and show me what he had found. I left my sister in the hot pool with Fox and his friends, sharing the second bottle of champagne, and followed my little white dog back to our new quarters.

"There's something tucked into the mattress," he said, once the door was closed. He sniffed at the edge of the mattress, and I poked my hand in a tiny hole and felt around with my fingers. The mattress was stuffed with something like kapok, and it came out in puffs. But eventually I felt some pieces of paper and pulled them out.

Unfortunately, it was hard to tell what they were. There was no light in the bedroom, except what came from the moon shining in the window, and there was little privacy in the bathroom. I finally locked myself in a stall. Pepe joined me by scooting under the door.

"It looks like a copy of a money order," I said at last. It was signed by Tammy and the amount was clear: $5,000. But the payee's name was not, although I could tell it started with a B. "I'm not sure this is important at all," I told Pepe. "This is probably just what Tammy paid for her beta-level training."

"But there is more than one," Pepe pointed out.

"That's true." They were all for the same amount and made out to the same payee, but there were five money orders with five different numbers.

"All in all, it adds up to twenty-five thousand dollars," I said. "This must be the money Mark was so upset about. But we still don't know if this is significant."

"If not, why would it be hidden?" Pepe asked.

"Good question," I said. "Maybe we should ask Jimmy G."

Chapter 28

The sun was just coming up as Pepe and I drove down toward Fern Lake to make our report to Jimmy G. The countryside was beautiful in the burgeoning light, but my mind was on other things—so much so that I took a turn too fast and almost ended up skidding into a tree.

"You have much on your mind, do you not, Geri?" Pepe asked.

"Yes, I do," I said. "First of all, I'm worried that Star is onto us. Maybe she knows we are PIs working this case undercover."

"*Que sera, sera,*" he said, adding Italian to his repertoire of foreign languages. "Even if she does, she has not acted upon it. As Dogawanda himself says, 'Bite only when there is something to sink your teeth into.'"

I laughed. "You've really been studying this stuff, haven't you?"

"Of course," my dog told me. "I want to be successful. What else is bothering you?"

"What is Artichoke going to do when I don't show up for my rock duty?" I asked.

"She will probably put you in the doghouse," said Pepe. When I did not laugh, he added, "That was a joke, Geri."

"I would not be surprised if they actually had a doghouse," I said.

"Is there something else?" Pepe wanted to know.

"Those money orders," I said. "Why would Tammy pay someone twenty-five thousand dollars?"

"Perhaps there is a training that costs that much."

"It's true," I said. "It may be that the next level costs twenty-five grand. But they don't seem to be made out to Crystal Star."

"Perhaps Crystal keeps it in a shell," Pepe said.

"A shell?" I was confused. "Oh, you mean like a shell corporation? Something set up to hide her assets."

"*Sí*, I heard about it on television," said Pepe.

"That's a good thought, Pepe," I said. "Let's check out the name again on the money orders and see if we can find it online. There must be Internet access in town."

Pepe stared out the window for a minute. "Do you know, Geri," he said, "I think there is something else bothering you."

"What would that be?"

"It is Felix. You fear that he will not believe you if you tell him that I can talk."

"Well, of course he won't believe me," I said. "Dogs don't talk."

"Except for me," he said. "And Dogawanda."

"Right, and Felix doesn't believe in Dogawanda. I'm not even sure that I do."

"Is it important to you that he believe you?"

"Yes," I said. "Wait! Are we talking about Dogawanda or Felix?"

"Felix, of course," he said. "And why is that important?"

"I don't know, Pepe," I said. "Maybe just that it's important to have someone else believe in you, even if their belief is misplaced."

"I must say, Geri, that it is *muy importante* to me that you listen to me. No one else ever has. And perhaps it is only because no one else believes it is possible."

"A good point, Pepe," I said. "I just have to convince Felix that it is possible for dogs to talk. That should be easy!"

"*Sí, muy facile*," agreed Pepe, who never gets my sarcasm.

Jimmy G was staying at an old motel on the outskirts of town called the Wagon Wheel. It was one of those old-fashioned motels, two stories and L-shaped, with doors arranged in a line. A giant wagon wheel sat propped up against a rock in front of the office and a huge trapezoid-shaped sign displayed the name in cursive letters.

Jimmy G had a room on the ground floor.

"Geri and rat-dog!" said Jimmy G expansively as he opened the door for us. "Come on in."

The room was fairly small and quite old, its walls paneled entirely with varnished knotty-pine. A double bed—with a rumpled blue comforter on it—occupied most of the room, except for an ancient TV with rabbit ears chained to a chest of drawers and an armchair that had seen better days in the far corner. The room reeked of cigar smoke. An almost-empty bottle of Jim Beam stood on the nightstand, two small water tumblers beside it.

"We're here," I told my boss as he closed the door behind us. "But we can't stay long. We've got to get back to the ranch before they miss us."

"Good news!" Jimmy G said, pulling out one of his ubiquitous cigars. "It turns out Jimmy G knows the town's sheriff!"

"Sheriff Pager?" I asked.

"Yeah. Ray was an MP at Fort Benning when Jimmy G took his jump training for the airborne division."

"I thought he said he was in supply in the army," Pepe told me.

"I thought you were in supply in the army, boss," I said.

"Never jumped. Fear of heights," he said, sitting on the bed and lighting up his stinky cigar. "That's why Jimmy G was in supply. Anyway, your boss saved Ray's bacon one night."

"That is a friend, indeed, who does not eat the bacon himself," said Pepe.

"Ray got jumped by three soldiers at a bar in town, and Jimmy G helped put the kibosh on them. Ray said he'd never forget it. So, here we are. Through serendipity, we got an in with local law enforcement. Got any aspirin with you?"

"Afraid not," I said.

"Oh well." The boss frowned. "Guess the only remedy is a little hair of the dog."

"Lay a hand on my fur and I will bite you severely!" Pepe warned.

Jimmy G poured the last of the whiskey into one of the tumblers, about two fingers' worth, then raised it to his lips, saying, "Down the hatch."

"He speaks *muy* strangely," said Pepe.

The boss drained the glass in one huge gulp. His face contorted as he shook his head and made a sound like a donkey braying. "There, that's better."

"If that is better," said Pepe, "I would not want to be worse."

"Have a seat," said Jimmy G. "Tell the boss about your progress."

I told him what I had learned from talking to my sister and Fox Black.

"Fox Black?" Jimmy G sat bolt upright and

grinned so wide I thought the corners of his mouth might tear. "He's here? Lead guitarist for The Spikes? Man, I listened to them all the way through Iraq. See if you can get Jimmy G an autograph."

"Well, I'll try—"

"Do more than try," the boss commanded. "Anyway, back to the case. You said they last saw the victim at around midnight."

"Yes."

"Interesting," said Jimmy G. "Because Ray said the coroner had finally established the time of death."

"And it is?"

"Approximately midnight."

"We need to find out what happened right after Fox left the hot springs," I said.

"Which means finding out who would have a motive to kill Tammy," Pepe added.

"Oh, that reminds me. We found these papers in Tammy's mattress," I said, pulling the copies of the money orders out of my pocket. I smoothed them out on the bureau. "Looks like the name is Broadbent. Maybe B. M. Broadbent?"

Jimmy G took the copies and peered at them, holding them up to a light as if looking for secret messages. "Now why does that sound familiar?"

"I don't know, boss," I said.

"Hey, I know," he said. "There was a guy drinking in the bar with us last night. Ray said he owns the local gas station. Introduced us. Said his name was Broadbent. Apparently his old man was the guy who founded Fern Lake."

"Why would Tammy be giving a money order to the guy who owns the gas station?" I asked.

"Don't ask Jimmy G! Maybe she was buying a gas station," Jimmy G said. "Tell you what, though. Ray was very impressed by the fact that Jimmy G had an operative in the compound. I'll pass this along to him. Meanwhile, Jimmy G will do some discreet sleuthing in town."

"Ha, discreet! Not likely with that tie!" Pepe was amused.

Jimmy G was wearing a bright red tie with crazy green and blue squiggles all over it. "What do you think of this?" he asked, holding it up.

"It's fine, boss," I told him, thinking that he was probably the only man in the world who actually wore all the bad ties that were perennially given as gifts.

"Yep. This is a good one," said Jimmy G. "If you spill ketchup on it, no one will notice."

"I think there *is* ketchup all over that tie," said Pepe, sniffing. Suddenly he darted under the bed. "Aha!" he exclaimed, dragging out a cellophane bag. "Half a bag of fried pork rinds!" It made crinkly noises as he pulled it along the carpet.

Jimmy G glanced down at the bag Pepe had in

his teeth. "Hey!" he said. "Those are Jimmy G's pork rinds!" He jumped to his feet. "Gimme!"

"No way, *hombre*," said Pepe, standing over the bag like it was a prized kill. "You will have to fight me for them. They are the next best thing to bacon!"

Chapter 29

"Is that not the stinky dogmobile?" Pepe asked as we headed for our car.

I looked across the street and saw the station wagon Felix uses for his dog-walking business parked on Main Street. It is an old Volvo station wagon outfitted with a screen between the front seats and the back so he can carry a number of dogs. Pepe had objected to sitting in the back like a mere dog.

"I wonder what he's doing in town?" I said. "I thought he was going up to the ranch to work with the wolf-dogs."

"Let us go investigate," said Pepe. "I will sniff him out."

His little nose led him to the front door of the police station. I pushed open the door and found both Felix and Tavo standing in the reception area, arguing with Alice.

"I'm sorry," Alice was saying. "There's nothing I

can do about it." She spotted me and Pepe at the door. "Geri," she said, "what are you doing here?"

Felix whirled around. He seemed happy to see me. "Geri!" he said. "Tell this woman I'm an animal trainer and expert on animal behavior. Tell her about the way those hybrids reacted when I got in their cage."

"It's true," I said to Alice. "He walked into their pen up at the ranch yesterday and they just laid down and practically worshipped him." And I could see why. He was looking really hot in a bright white cotton T-shirt and a pair of tight black jeans.

"It doesn't matter what they did," said Alice. "They've been impounded as dangerous animals and they're going to be put down."

"But we need them for the movie!" Tavo said after giving me a big smile. "Can't you postpone their execution until we get this straightened out?"

"It's not up to me," said Alice. "You'd have to talk to the animal safety officer."

"And where's he?" I asked.

"He's out on a call," she said.

"Where are the wolf-dogs?" I asked.

"They're at the vet's office. That's where we keep the impounded animals."

"Where is the vet?" I asked Alice.

"Over on Second Street," she said. "But he won't be able to release the animals. Not without permission from the sheriff."

"What if I can prove the hybrids did not attack anyone?" Felix asked.

"How would you do that?" Alice wanted to know. I wanted to know, too.

"I could compare the marks on the body to the animal's actual paws, plus look at the crime scene photos to determine how the attack occurred—if it occurred."

"He's been an expert witness at trials on animal attacks," Tavo said. That was something I didn't know about Felix. Impressive.

"He's known as the Wolf Whisperer," I added.

Felix winced. Tavo looked amused. "Wolf Whisperer?" he repeated, then regained his composure. "Yes, indeed, the one and only Wolf Whisperer."

Alice seemed persuaded by this title to call the sheriff for approval for Felix to examine Tammy's body, so Pepe and I volunteered to head over to the vet's office to check on the wolf-dogs, while Tavo and Felix headed to the mortuary to meet the sheriff.

We headed down Main Street, past the bar, and turned right onto a street of little houses. The first one on the left, a little blue cottage, had a big wooden sign in front saying COIFFURES BY CARRIE. The second one, which was a faded peach color, had a sign hanging above the front steps reading FRANK FORREST, DVM.

We clattered up the steps and in through the front door, which was unlocked. The living room had been converted into a waiting room. The floor was covered with lime-green linoleum, which smelled of antiseptic and urine. Long benches covered with brown Naugahyde lined the walls. But there were no patients.

There were taxidermy animals, which seemed odd to me in a vet's office. A giant owl perched above the door that led to the reception counter. A stuffed beaver stood holding a bell that sported a little sign asking me to ring for service. So I did.

There was no response. I rang again. The beaver swayed a little. Pepe was dancing around, and I knew he didn't have to pee because he had watered the posts holding up the sign in front. Maybe it was all the taxidermy animals making him nervous.

"Something bad is happening, Geri," he said. "I smell fear. We must get in there."

"OK! If you say so!" I pushed through the hinged door that separated the waiting room from the rest of the house. We found ourselves in a big room lined with shelves. In the center was a large stainless-steel table, and one of the wolf-dogs lay on it, sprawled on its side, its legs sticking straight out, its bushy tail hanging down, almost brushing the floor. A short, balding man in a white coat was bending over the wolf with a syringe in his hand.

"Oh my God!" I said, not entirely pretending to be alarmed. "That looks like a wolf!"

"It is a hybrid," said the vet, looking up. He seemed to be pleased. "Very dangerous animal. Attacked and killed a woman up at the Dogawanda ranch."

"What are you going to do to him?" I asked.

"I just sedated him, and now I'm going to administer a cocktail that will put him to sleep forever."

"Geri! We must do something!" Pepe said.

"I know, but what?" I asked him.

"I know!" said Pepe, and fell over on his side. "Ow! Ow! Ow!" he said, rolling around on the floor, waving his little feet back and forth.

"Oh my God!" I said. "My dog is having a seizure."

"Is he really?" The vet looked at him suspiciously. "That was sudden."

"That's the way they happen," I said. "One minute he's fine. The next he's like this. That's why I brought him in. I could sense this was about to happen."

Pepe flopped around like a fish, his tongue hanging out of his mouth.

The vet frowned. "Well, I can examine him in a minute. Put him on the table over there." He pointed to another table set against the wall, under a glass-fronted cabinet, then bent back over the wolf-dog, the syringe raised. I saw my chance and stumbled forward, pretending to be lunging for Pepe but knocking the syringe out of his hand. It bounced on the floor and rolled under a cabinet.

"Damn it!" said the vet. He peered under the cabinet as I scooped Pepe up and put him on the table.

"Now what?" I asked him, but the vet thought I was talking to him.

"The sedative should wear off in about ten minutes," he said, glancing at the wolf-dog. "I hope this won't take too long." He hunched over Pepe, grabbing his jaws and forcing them open. Pepe's long pink tongue flopped out of his mouth. He rolled his eyes as far back in his head as he could. He definitely looked like a dog in distress.

"I think he needs a shot," said the vet, putting one of his hands firmly down on top of Pepe's small body and groping with his other hand in the drawer underneath the counter.

"No, Geri, no!" yelled Pepe. He began struggling. "Don't let him give me a shot!"

"My dog is afraid of shots," I said, stepping forward.

"He won't feel a thing," said the vet, pulling out a plastic pack that contained a syringe and sticking it in his teeth. He ripped it open by pulling on the other end.

Oh my God! What was I going to do?

Pepe was making a terrible squeaking sound.

"Hold it!" said a strong masculine voice. I turned to see the sheriff in the doorway and behind him were Felix and Tavo.

Chapter 30

"What are you doing here?" I asked, so grateful to see them.

"New wrinkle in the case, Frank," the sheriff said to the vet.

Frank let go of Pepe. He leaped off the table. I was always surprised by how far he could jump without injury.

"*Gracias*, amigo!" he said with a little bow to Felix. And then he turned to me, putting a little paw on my foot, which was a signal to pick him up. "Finally your *novio* has proved his value," he said, licking my cheek.

"Looks like you're OK now, little guy," I said, kissing him on the top of his head.

"That was a fast recovery," the vet said with a frown.

"A miracle!" I said.

The vet dropped the syringe into a plastic

container on the counter and turned to the sheriff. "Who are these people?"

"I work for a production company and we have a contract with the Dogawanda Center allowing us to use these animals in a movie," Tavo said, pointing at the wolf-dog. "We came to get them. If we can't use them, the contract will be voided and we will have the right to sue you for the cost of replacing them."

"Dash it all!" said the vet. He looked at the sheriff. "Those weirdos are always interfering with us." He stood in front of the wolf-dog, rolling up his sleeves as if getting ready for a fight. "Anyway, the contract doesn't matter. Last night these wolves attacked a woman."

"Looks like that might not be true," said the sheriff reluctantly. "We just went over to the mortuary and looked at the body. This young fellow—" He waved his hand at Felix.

"The Wolf Whisperer!" said Tavo with a snicker in his voice.

"—examined the marks on the body. Don't know why I didn't see it before. Clearly not the marks one would associate with an attack. No gouging. No gnawing. No attempt to cache the body."

"Maybe they don't behave like wild animals," the vet suggested. "After all, they are being kept as pets."

"Look," Felix told the vet, "there weren't even any bite marks on the body. No puncture wounds at all. The only marks on her body were abrasions and scratches. But they weren't consistent with a wolf attack in any way, shape, or form."

"Frank, I made a mistake," the sheriff told the vet. "These animals might be dangerous, but they did not attack that woman up at the compound."

"Maybe the other animal did?" the vet suggested.

"He really does seem eager to kill them," Pepe suggested. "Perhaps he wants to stuff them!"

"There is no way in hell," said Felix, sounding irritated, "that one of these hybrids killed her. You might as well blame Crystal Star's old Weimaraner."

"I'm glad they are not blaming me," Pepe told me. "We Chihuahuas are known for our ferocity. But I do have an alibi, just in case."

The sedated wolf-dog was beginning to wake up. His paws twitched lightly.

"What do you want me to do, then?" Frank asked the sheriff. "You want me to let these animals go?"

"I can guarantee that they will be confined and carefully monitored," Felix said. "And since I don't believe the conditions at the Dogawanda Center are suitable for long-term care, I will make arrangements to have the animals placed in a center where they will be able to live more natural lives without any danger to the general populace."

"That sounds good to me!" said the sheriff, shaking his hand. "Kills two birds with one stone." He turned to the vet. "You can release them into this man's custody. See that it's done."

He and the vet helped Felix and Tavo load the sedated wolf into the back of the "stinky dog-mobile." Then the sheriff left and we went back inside to get the other wolf-dog, which was in the outside kennel.

To get there, we had to go through a small back room. There were cages stacked along one wall. One contained a sleepy gray Persian cat who raised his heavy head, examined us, and then turned around, showing off his magnificent bushy tail. The only other occupant of the kennel was a little dirty white dog. She was looking out through the bars, her dark eyes bright and whimpering softly.

"Geri, it is Fuzzy!" said Pepe, stopping abruptly and looking up at the little dog.

"Fuzzy?" I said. I peered through the grate at the animal inside the kennel, and it did appear to be the dirty little white dog I had last seen at Mark Darling's house, only much dirtier. She whimpered softly.

"Are you sure?" I asked Pepe.

"I never forget a smell," he said.

"You know this dog?" the vet asked.

"She belonged to Tammy Darling, the woman who died," I said. "How long has she been here?"

The vet looked at the tag on the cage. "She was picked up Saturday afternoon around two p.m. Wandering along the highway."

"Do you suppose she walked all the way from Seattle?" I asked. "Mark said she went missing around midnight on Friday."

"Which was around the time Tammy died," Pepe pointed out.

"Let me look at her paws!" Felix suggested.

"Can we take her out?" I asked.

The vet nodded.

I pinched the latch so the door opened and Fuzzy practically fell into my arms, licking my face with enthusiasm.

Felix picked up Fuzzy's paw. He shook his head. "She did not walk all the way here from Seattle. Her paws would be in much worse shape."

"So can we take her?" I asked the vet.

He shook his head. "Not unless you're the owner."

"But the owner is dead," I said.

"Who's her next of kin?"

"Well, I suppose her husband, but he's in Seattle."

"And besides, he does not seem to care for *perros* much," said Pepe.

"He needs to be the one to get her out," the vet said. He seemed determined.

"What if he's not interested in getting her back?" I asked.

"Well, he can either sign her over to you or you have to wait for the three-day waiting period and then come in and pay the adoption fee."

"I suppose I could do that," I said. Reluctantly I put the little dog back into her cage.

"Fuzzy, never fear, we will rescue you," said Pepe. To me, he said, "We must plan a *perro* prison break, Geri. It is not safe to leave her in the hands of someone who likes to stuff animals."

Chapter 31

Felix loaded the other wolf-dog into his car, and he and Tavo took off for the Dogawanda ranch. But Pepe and I had one more errand to run. I was determined to talk to B. M. Broadbent and find out why Tammy was giving him money.

We went into the gas station—Pepe insisted I buy him some beef jerky—and I asked where I could find Mr. Broadbent. The cashier told me he had an office over at the city hall.

We found city hall easy enough. It was located up the block across the street from the bar. It wasn't very large. It looked more like a small house than my idea of a city hall. It was painted white and had a steeply angled metal roof that shone brightly in the sun. An American flag flew from a pole that stuck out over the place's small front porch.

There was no reception desk in the small foyer, just a large sign on the wall facing us—black with white plastic, stick-on letters—that listed the respective offices of the mayor and the three members of the town council.

"There," I said, "Barrett Matthew Broadbent the Third, that's who we want to see."

"Why the *Third*?" asked Pepe.

"Well, I suppose his grandfather was first, and his father was second. That would make him the third."

"I fail to see why anyone would advertise being in third place," Pepe said with a disdainful wrinkle of his nose. "On the other hand, I would definitely enjoy being known as Pepe Sullivan the First."

"Oh, indeed, sir," I agreed, curtsying. "Would you deign to accompany your lowly subject to the councilman's office?"

As usual, he didn't get my sarcasm, just said, "Lead the way."

We went down the short hall, Pepe's nails clicking on the scuffed hardwood flooring. The first door we came to was marked with a brass plaque that read OFFICE OF THE MAYOR—HENRY "HANK" DAVENPORT. The door was closed, and I didn't hear any sounds of activity behind it.

The same was true of the next two doors we passed, belonging to town council members Randy Peterson and Evelyn Meyers. (I did note, with some satisfaction, that at least one of the civic leaders was female.)

Approaching the last door at the end of the hall, Pepe said, "I do not hear the sounds of any people in this place. What if nobody is here?"

I hadn't considered that we might not find anybody at the city hall. If our guy wasn't in, I—

"Wait!" said Pepe. "Hear that?"

"Yes."

"*Musica*," he said.

It was music. The old country song "Your Cheatin' Heart." It was coming from the last door, which had to be Broadbent's office.

"I believe it is the original," observed Pepe. "By Hank Williams."

"Since when were you into country western?" I asked.

"I only like the classic stuff," he told me.

Just another thing I didn't know about my dog.

I went to the door and checked the brass plaque on it before knocking. It was indeed Broadbent's office. Below his extremely long name, the plaque also was inscribed with, WELCOME CONSTITUENTS! COME ON IN AND SAY HI TO BARRY!

"This is what is called an open-door policy, is it not?" Pepe asked me.

"I suppose you're right."

"Then why is the door closed?"

I shook my head, saying, "Don't ask," and knocked on the door.

We heard someone shout, "Come on in!" and so we did. The office would have been your typical government cubicle—white blinds, steel-gray metal desk, beige file cabinets—except for the mounted deer heads and rifle racks that lined the walls.

A tall, husky man somewhere in his midforties

was sitting at the desk. He had carroty red hair, cut in a flattop, and a big smile. He got up as we entered and approached me with his hand out. He was wearing a red, Western-style shirt (the kind with pearl snaps instead of buttons on it) and a pair of crisp Levi's with a huge, silver belt buckle adorning a wide tooled-leather belt.

"Watch it," Pepe warned me. "I think this is called glad-handing."

"Barrett Matthew Broadbent the Third," he said, his oversized hand swallowing mine whole. "Just call me Barry. To whom do I have the pleasure?"

"Whatever you are selling, we are not buying," said Pepe.

"Geri," I told him, wondering when I'd get my hand back. "Geri Sullivan."

"Glad to meet you," Barry said, using my hand like a pump handle, then finally releasing it. "And you've brought your little dog with you, I see."

"I hope you don't mind," I said.

"Mind?" he said, kneeling down in front of Pepe. "Not on your life. I love dogs. Got a few myself. What's your name, little guy?" he asked Pepe.

"Trouble," Pepe told him with a curl of his lip.

"Spunky, isn't he?" Barry said, standing up again. "So, what brings you to me, Miss Sullivan? It is *Miss*, isn't it?" he asked, glancing at the ringless third finger of my left hand.

"Yes," I told him. As to his question of why I came to see him, I just said, "Well . . ." and paused, wondering how to answer. (*The Private Detective's Bible* said to try and put a suspect at ease in order to get them talking.) "Are you a hunter?" I continued, looking past him at the gun rack on the wall behind his desk. "That's quite a collection of guns you have."

Barry smiled, taking it as a compliment. "Yup. My daddy hunted and my grandpa before him," he said. "You hunt?"

"We hunt criminals," said Pepe.

"Not really," I told him. "But I've always had a deep appreciation of firearms." *The Private Detective's Bible* made it clear a little white lie was acceptable when questioning a suspect.

Barry nodded, then went to the gun rack and took one of his rifles out of it. "You'll like this one, then," he said, bringing it over to me.

Even with my limited knowledge of guns, I recognized it as the kind of rifle that cowboys always used in old Western movies.

Barry pulled the rifle's lever down—to make sure it wasn't loaded, I think—then handed the rifle to me, saying, "Try this on for size. It's an 1873 Winchester Commemorative, hundredth anniversary limited edition. Belonged to my father." The councilman pointed to the stuffed animal heads on the wall. "He took that eight-point buck there with it. I took the six-pointer beside it with the same gun. Sweet deer rifle the thirty-thirty."

"He is a killer of defenseless animals," said Pepe.

"What do you think?" Barry asked me.

"It's lovely," I said, looking the rifle over. I hefted

it and looked down its barrel like I knew what I was doing. I handed it back to him, saying, "You must be proud to own it."

"Sure enough," he said, placing the rifle back in the rack. "Have a seat," he added, turning from the gun rack and sitting down at his desk.

There were two small leather chairs in front of the desk. Pepe jumped up on one, so I sat down on the other.

Barry clasped his hands on the desk pad in front of him. "You're not from around these parts, are you, Miss Sullivan?" he asked. "You just in town for the day or—"

"No, I'm here for a while."

"Good," he said. "Staying down at the resort, I imagine?"

"Yes," I lied.

"On vacation?"

"Sort of."

"Sort of?"

I figured it was time to start getting down to business. "Actually I'm here doing research on the Dogawandans," I told him.

"*Them?*" He said it as if I were talking about cockroaches. "The *Dogawandans?*"

"Why, yes," I said. "You seem shocked by that. Have you had any trouble with them?"

"Well, yes and no," said Barry. "Their ideas and the town's ideas haven't exactly matched from time to time. They like to get their own way. Council's been working with them, though. Takes all kinds, you know. They *have* brought some extra business to town since they got here. I'll give them that."

"So that's good, right?"

"Sure enough. We're just a little mountain town in the middle of nowhere to most folks. But we're starting to grow again. Like the big resort you're staying at. Now *that* has really increased the town's revenues. So much so, I'm happy to say, that I'm about to remodel my gas station into a convenience store type station like you see in the bigger cities."

"Really?" I asked. "I imagine that's pretty costly."

"Yup. But my business model shows that it should work out nicely. It will be well worth it."

I'd gotten him relaxed and talkative like *The Private Detective's Bible* said you should, so now was the time to spring the direct question on him.

"And the twenty-five thousand dollars you got from Tammy Darling," I said in the friendliest sort of manner, "will sure help with expanding your gas station, won't it?"

"Sure will," he said. "I—" He abruptly stopped talking. His expression went all gargoyle-like and he said, *"What did you say?"*

"You heard her, mister!" said Pepe.

Now was the time I was supposed to be hard and tough in my questioning. "How did you know Tammy Darling, Councilman Broadbent?"

"What?" His face turned beet red.

"And why would she give you that kind of money?"

"I don't even"—he began to fidget—"know who you're talking about."

"Don't play games with me," I said in my best hard-boiled voice, thinking this was going really well, just like *The Private Detective's Bible* suggested it would.

"Who *are* you?" asked Barry, raising his voice.

"That is for us to know, and you to find out," said Pepe. "Now spill it!"

"I have copies of the money orders Tammy signed," I told the councilman.

"It was just, uh, a campaign contribution," he said. "For the next election, that's all."

"Why would Tammy contribute to your campaign?" I asked.

The councilman jumped to his feet. "It was a totally legitimate transaction and I don't have to answer your questions. This conversation is over."

"If that's the way you want it," I said.

"Out!" he said, coming around the desk, flailing his arms. "Get out or I'll throw you—"

Pepe said, "I think we better *vamoose.*"

He didn't have to say it twice. I almost knocked my chair over as I got up and reached for the doorknob. As Pepe and I headed down the hall, we heard the sounds of swearing and stomping and something breaking behind us.

Reaching safety half a block up from city hall, with Councilman Broadbent thankfully nowhere in sight, Pepe said, "Geri, perhaps we should consider refining our interrogation technique a bit."

Where I'd gone wrong, I didn't know, but before I could agree with him, Mark Darling came charging up the street. He was wearing a yellow polo shirt and crisply pressed khaki pants. He was also breathing fire when he reached us.

"What are you doing here?" I asked.

"I'm looking for Councilman Broadbent!" he yelled at me. "Where is he?"

"He's in city hall," I said. "We just saw him."

"And?"

"And what?" I asked.

"Did you get my money?"

"No," I told him. "The councilman—"

"Well I'll damn sure get it!"

Mark turned to go, but I grabbed him by the arm. "Wait," I said. "How do you know about him having your money?"

"Your boss, Jimmy G, told me. What do you think?"

"Oh, right . . . of course," I said, wishing Jimmy G hadn't shared our conversation with Mark.

"What kind of private detectives are you, anyway?" He pulled away from me. "That's what I hired you for! But never mind! I'll get it myself!" He barreled up the street. "And that means you won't get any."

"Mark!" I called after him, to no avail. "Mark!" I yelled as loud as I could, but he was already mounting the steps to city hall.

"I would not go in there just now!!" Pepe called to him.

Chapter 32

"Do you think we should go back in there and rescue him?" I asked Pepe, watching as Mark pulled the door open and marched inside.

"I think we should go enlist the help of our boss," said Pepe.

The motel was only a few blocks from the city hall, and we hurried over there, looking back occasionally to see if Mark had emerged from the encounter, which I half expected.

Jimmy G was in his room. A great puff of cigar smoke floated out as he opened the door, along with the voice of Judge Judy, who was castigating some poor litigant on the TV.

"What's up, doll?" Jimmy G asked, removing his cigar from his mouth.

"I just saw Mark Darling," I said, "and I think he might need our help. He was going to confront Broadbent—"

"The third," Pepe added.

"Don't interrupt," I said.

"Jimmy G wasn't interrupting," said our boss.

I decided to ignore both of them. "—and the guy was not in a good mood. Plus his office is full of guns."

"And the stuffed heads of helpless animals that he slaughtered," said Pepe, shivering.

"Hey, don't you worry your pretty little head, sweetheart," said our boss. "Mark Darling can take care of himself. Besides, he fired us."

"What? How did that happen?" I asked.

"He stormed in all indignant because he said Jimmy G and his operatives weren't doing their job. Jimmy G showed him that piece of paper you and your rat-dog had found up at the compound."

"So that's what set him off?" I asked.

"When he found out his wife had given twenty-five grand to this Broadbent character, he wanted to know why. Told him Jimmy G couldn't read minds and maybe he should go talk to Dogawanda if he wanted an answer. That's when he marched out of here and said if we weren't going to do our jobs, he would do it for us!"

"That was our only piece of evidence," I said.

"And we *were* doing our jobs," Pepe said.

"Well, actually I think maybe we blew it," I told Jimmy G. "I was questioning Broadbent, trying to get him to explain what the money was for and instead of getting information, I just got him all riled up."

"Like poking a bear," said Pepe.

"Funny metaphor," I said, looking at my dog.

"Never did understand what 'riled' meant," admitted Jimmy G. "So tell me more about your interrogation techniques."

"Well, they came straight out of *The Private Detective's Bible*," I said. "You know, where you're supposed to start out friendly and then drop in a zinger—"

Jimmy G cut me off. "You're just too cute to use that technique, doll. Dames got to work the interview from a different angle. Use your feminine wiles. Get him eating out of your hand."

"Well, if that is the case, then you really blew it, Geri," Pepe said.

We headed back up to the ranch, leaving Jimmy G to deal with the brouhaha over the money orders.

When we arrived at the compound, I saw Felix's car in the parking lot but it was empty. He and Tavo must have unloaded the wolf-dogs and perhaps they were putting them back in their pen.

I felt a little guilty about being gone for so long—at the beta level, Dogawandans were not supposed to leave the compound at all—but there was no one at the Beta Barn when I returned. I slipped into my new Dogawandan clothes and went

out looking for them, meanwhile trying to think of
a great excuse for my absence. The lack of caffeine
was still bothering me, and I decided I would
simply say I went into town to get some medicine
for my headache.

The kitchen was humming as Dogawandans
prepared for lunch. I asked one of the women tearing up kale where to find everyone else.

"They're in the Longhouse, preparing for the
memorial," she said.

"Memorial?"

She looked at me sternly. "For Leaf!"

"Oh, of course."

"We're preparing the funeral feast. As Dogawanda prescribes, everything must be alive to
symbolize the new life that Leaf will live on the
other side."

I nodded as if I understood.

"Do you suppose they noticed my absence?" I
asked Pepe.

"I'm sure they noticed mine," he said. He
sounded forlorn. "How can Crystal channel Dogawanda without me?"

"Perhaps she doesn't need to channel Dogawanda to prepare for a memorial," I said, trying to
reassure my suddenly needy dog.

The Dogawandan thought I was talking to her.
"Crystal and Dogawanda have already consulted on
the choreography of the service. Now she is simply
explaining it to all of the others."

"Should we go join them?"

"I wouldn't," she said. "Not unless you want to get called out in front of everyone for dereliction of duty. With any luck, you can join the group when everyone assembles for the memorial," the woman said, going back to her task. "Just listen for the bell."

Chapter 33

Since we had some free time on our hands, I decided to check in with Felix and find out how the wolf-dogs were adjusting to their reprieve.

"I do not understand the point of that," grumbled Pepe, but he followed me as I left the kitchen and took the path into the woods. The feeble sunlight dwindled and dimmed, but with Pepe charging ahead we were able to retrace our steps and arrive at the wolf pen, where we found Felix and Tavo and the two wolf-dogs. One of the animals was lying on the ground at Tavo's feet, apparently still asleep.

Felix had the other wolf-dog on a long leash, with a muzzle over its snout. The wolf-dog shook its head back and forth, trying to shake off the strange contraption attached to its face.

There was a third person on the scene: Chloe, who was dressed more sensibly than the last time I had seen her, in jeans and a camisole top. But she was still shivering, and it was unclear if it was from fear or cold, since she was half hiding behind Felix.

"Keep it away from me!" she shrieked.

"She's not going to hurt you!" Felix said. He sounded annoyed.

"She can't open her mouth," said Tavo.

"Hi, Geri," said Felix, looking up and seeing me. "We've got the hybrids back safely, but now we have to see if we can work with them. They've both been traumatized by their incarceration." He looked at Tavo. "I'm not sure we can have them ready by tomorrow."

"We've got to, bro," Tavo said. "The whole crew is already on the way up here. We're scheduled to shoot the scenes with the wolves tomorrow night."

"I know, Tav," said Felix, "but look at them. I can't guarantee anyone's safety"—Chloe shrieked and clutched Felix tighter—"without the muzzle, but I'm not sure I can get her used to it by tomorrow and the other animal"—he pointed at the slumbering wolf-dog—"is still sedated."

"Poor thing," I said, kneeling down and putting my hands on either side of the wolf-dog's snout, lifting it up toward my nose as I often do with Pepe when he's slumbering.

"Geri! No!" Felix dropped the leash he was holding and lunged at me, pushing me aside so roughly, I fell sideways into the dirt. He stood over me, his face contorted with such rage I was afraid he was going to strike me. I cowered like a submissive dog.

Luckily, Pepe was not submissive. He jumped in

front of me and began growling. Meanwhile, Chloe was screaming and running around in circles, flapping her arms while the suddenly liberated wolf-dog dashed into the underbrush.

"Good grief, Geri!" said Felix, yanking me to my feet. "Don't you ever do that again!"

"Unhand her, you brute!" said Pepe, circling around Felix's ankles. Knowing him, he was looking for the right place to attack. Lucky for Felix he was wearing cowboy boots. Pepe has a fondness for Achilles tendons.

"What?" I said. "He looked so peaceful." Indeed, the slumbering wolf-dog had not responded to any of the screaming and shrieking.

"You better tell her what's going on, Felix," Tavo said. "But first you're missing a wolf!"

"Damn!" said Felix, looking around and noticing for the first time that his other wolf-dog was gone. Chloe was still wandering around in circles, but now she was whimpering.

"Stop it!" said Felix. "You're acting like prey! You're lucky the wolf didn't turn on you!" I had never seen him quite so angry. In fact, I had never seen him angry.

"Cool it, bro," said Tavo. "I'll take care of Chloe. You go get that wolf before we lose it."

"I will help," said Pepe, putting his nose to the ground and dashing off in the direction the wolf-dog had gone.

"Come back here, Pepe!" I yelled. But he was off, with Felix following close behind him.

"What's going on?" I asked Tavo.

"It's a long story," he said, "and one you have to hear from Felix." He turned to Chloe. "Come on, I'll take you back to the car." But first, he half dragged the slumbering wolf-dog to the pen and shut it inside. I wasn't sure why he was allowed to get so close to a sleeping wolf-dog while I wasn't. My ego was really bruised.

I decided to follow Felix and Pepe. Apparently it was something I did that had upset Felix and that had caused the wolf-dog to bolt. Plus my dog was missing. In the woods! With a wild wolf!

I headed in the direction where I could hear Pepe's voice calling out directions. "Over here, Felix!" and "Circle around behind her." But since Felix couldn't hear Pepe, I didn't know how it would help. At some times it sounded like Pepe was talking to the wolf-dog. "Calm down. We come in peace."

The sound seemed to come first from one direction, then another. And my path was equally unclear, blocked by a fallen tree, too big for me to scramble over. When I tried to go around it, brambles snagged my shirt. Soon I could no longer hear Pepe.

The air was cool between the big trees. I stopped and realized I had no idea where I was. I remembered something from Girl Scouts. The moss on the trees would tell me which direction was north, so I studied the trunks of the tall trees around me. The jagged bark of the pines had patches of moss, and I thought I could discern a pattern. If the moss could be relied on, I was somewhere north, or higher up the mountain than the Dogawandan compound and needed to head downhill. I began to move in that direction, stopping frequently to pick a path over outcrops of rock and rotting trunks of fallen trees, pushing aside prickly salal and the leathery green leaves of fern.

Just as I was beginning to lose faith in my progress, and thinking I had perhaps seen that particular boulder before, I heard a strange sound: a crescendo of howls that raised the hair on the back of my neck. It must be coming from the Dogawandan ranch. I pressed forward and was rewarded by seeing more light between the trees. Eventually I stepped out into a clear space and saw that I was right on the edge of the woods, behind the lodge. The Dogawandans were gathering around the fire pit. Something was happening and I needed to know what.

Just then I heard Pepe's voice.

"Geri! I found you!" He raced toward me. I stooped down to scoop him into my arms.

Felix was right behind him.

"Geri, thank God! You're safe!" he said, rushing toward me and pulling me into an embrace. "Your dog is such a good tracker. He brought me straight to you. It was almost like following Lassie."

"What about the wolf-dog?" I asked.

"The leash got tangled in the brush pretty quickly," said Felix. "She wasn't far. Just freaked out. Pepe helped there, too. He seemed able to calm her down by his presence. She's safe, back in the pen."

"I talked to her," said Pepe. "She responded well to the precepts of Dogawanda."

"And Towering Cedar," I said.

"What?"

"Pepe's Dogawandan name," I said.

"He's a marvel," said Felix, patting Pepe on the head.

"Geri, we must hurry!" said Pepe. "Dogawanda needs us!"

I set him down. "Pepe and I need to participate in this, whatever it is."

"I know. I'm sorry, Geri." Felix shook his head. His dark eyes were pleading. "I behaved badly. I'm really embarrassed. I need to explain what happened."

"It's OK," I said. "I understand you were worried about me."

"Come on, Geri," said Pepe, trotting toward the gathering.

"It's more than that," Felix said. "It's complicated. But it's important."

"I want to listen," I said. "I really do. But—" I looked at Pepe as he reached the edge of the circle and another howl went up. "I really need to figure out what's going on here. Can we talk later?"

Felix looked crestfallen. "I guess."

"Where will you be?" I asked.

"The film company booked a bunch of rooms at

the resort," Felix said. He fumbled in his pocket and pulled out a room key: a plastic card tucked inside a paper sheath that was imprinted with the number 602. "Here's my extra room key."

"OK, I'll see you there later," I said. He gave me a quick hug and I turned and ran off after my dog.

Chapter 34

The Dogawandans stood in circles around the fire pit, right in front of the Lodge. They were arranged, as they usually were, by level. I could see Terry in the first circle, right next to Crystal and Fox Black, who had a guitar slung over his shoulder. We took our place in the very last row.

"Hold me up so I can see," Pepe told me.

I held him up. "Can you see now?" I asked.

"Uh-huh," he said. "Look at that—Fox Black has his famous Gibson Hummingbird with him."

"Since when did you become an expert on guitars?" I asked my dog.

He looked me square in the eye and tilted his head as he replied, "Everybody knows that *Senor* Black has his favorite guitar. It is legend."

"Oh," I said.

"Besides, I know all about guitars. I once traveled with some of the best Tex-Mex bands. How do you think I learned to dance?"

"Welcome all," said Crystal, spreading her arms. Then she held one hand out, palm down, and gestured toward the ground. "Sit!" she commanded.

On cue, everyone sat cross-legged, Pepe and I following suit.

"That is an easy trick for a dog," he said.

"On this solemn but joyous occasion," Crystal intoned, "we celebrate the life and passing of our beloved Leaf." She paused and nodded with a warm smile. "But know this: her passing was but a passing from this Now to the Eternal Now. All praise to Dogawanda."

"All praise to Dogawanda," chanted the assembled devotees.

"Before we begin our procession to the spot where Leaf last fell," said Crystal, "our fellow enlightened one, Fox Black, has written and will perform a song in her honor."

Crystal stepped back and Fox stepped forward.

"You all know," Fox continued, "that I have had my share of troubles." One of his bandmates had died of an overdose and it was well known that Fox had been thrown out of the band several times because of his own drug use. "But thanks to Dogawanda, I am able to be here with you, free of my compulsions, thanks to the freedom of perfect obedience to the Now." Fox continued, one hand resting on the guitar's body. "*Now* is where it's at!"

"*Now!*" came the unified reply.

"So this song is for Leaf," Fox continued. "It's

called 'A Tree Has Many Leaves.'" He strummed the guitar and began to sing:

> "The leaf is free
> It falls from the tree
> Down through the woods
> To the roots of the tree
> Where it rots and becomes
> The food of the roots
> It becomes the tree
> And the tree bears leaves
> All is Dogawanda
> There is no death
> Only life
> The circle of life
> It never ends."

"No wonder Dogawanda told him to focus on guitar-playing and not songwriting," said Pepe.

"So beautiful," said the woman next to me. She dabbed at her wet eyes.

Fox bowed his head and stepped back as Crystal came to the forefront once again.

"We thank you, Fox," she said. "Dogawanda thanks you." She put one hand out toward us, then raised it quickly. "Up!" she ordered.

We all stood again.

"I am glad her command was 'up' instead of 'roll over,'" said Pepe. "I will never do that one. It is too degrading."

"We are going to create a memorial to Leaf,"

Crystal said. "All things exist in time, but for a rock, time passes more slowly than for a plant or an animal. So we will build our memorial out of stone. As we proceed to the place where she passed from the Now into the Eternal Now, I encourage you to pick up a rock, a rock of sufficient weight to represent the sorrow you feel at Leaf's passing, so that when you put it down on the spot where she fell, you will lay down any grief or any regrets as well."

The Dogawandans formed a loose line, with the inner pack up at the front as usual, which meant that Pepe and I were at the rear. We moved slowly along the path to the front gate and then out across the parking lot. As we passed the area at the edge of the parking lot where the rocks were deposited, everyone stopped and began searching for a rock.

"Put me down, Geri. There are rocks all over—I want to get one for Leaf, too."

"That's sweet," I said, and put him on the ground. He started casting about for a rock like everyone else was doing.

"Here is the perfect size for me," said Pepe, standing over a rock that seemed bigger than his mouth.

"Do you want me to carry it for you?" I asked. I wasn't sure if he could manage to open his jaws wide enough to scoop it up. Meanwhile, most of the Dogawandans seemed to have settled on a rock and were starting off again, following Crystal down the dirt road that led to the construction site.

"I can do it myself," said Pepe, scooping up the rock and taking off after them.

I grabbed the biggest rock I could see and ran after him, staggering a little under the weight of the heavy piece of granite.

I couldn't see Pepe. Knowing him, he had dashed ahead to the front of the line. I fell in with the others, processing in single file along the dirt road that led from the parking lot to the construction site.

As we came out into the open space, I saw that the Dogawandans who were at the front of the line had gathered in a circle around the place where we had found Leaf's body. They must have placed their rocks and then stepped back to admire their handiwork. Oddly enough, they were moaning and crying. Some were turning their heads away. Others were clutching each other. Perhaps this was all part of the ceremony. A release of emotion.

I tried to push forward, determined to get to the front of the circle and to find my dog. Pepe dashed up to me. He seemed frantic. He was trying to speak, but he couldn't because of the rock in his mouth. So his words came out as "Grrsh, dosh rawr."

I knelt down and removed the rock from his mouth, which meant setting my stone aside, and he spoke again: "Geri, don't go any farther!"

"What? Why not?" The Dogawandans were moving away. I could see that something was lying on the ground. It wasn't a pile of rocks. It was a body. I got up, unable to believe what I was seeing, and moved forward for a better look.

The body belonged to a man. One shoe had been removed and his toe was jammed into the trigger of a rifle. It looked familiar. It looked like the rifle Broadbent had handed me just a few hours earlier. The gun lay across the body with the barrel pointed at the head, but you couldn't make out any features because the face was splattered with blood. But I didn't need to see the face to know who lay there. I recognized the yellow polo shirt and immaculately pressed khaki pants.

"It's Mark Darling!" I said.

Chapter 35

Back to the Fern Lake police station we went.

"It is beginning to feel like home," said Pepe.

My dog was obviously unhappy about being dragged in for questioning once again. I'm sure the same held true for all the Dogawandans.

"Why does everybody have to give a statement?" asked Pepe. "We all saw the same thing."

"The sheriff is just being thorough," I told him. "Even when it's the same thing, everyone sees it differently."

"I suppose that is true," said Pepe. "If you and I see a pig, you see a pig, but I see bacon. And if you and I see a cow, you see a cow but I see a cheeseburger."

"Enough already. I get your point."

"I was only agreeing with you," he said. "Don't be so touchy."

"Sorry." I gave him a pat on the head, realizing I

was being a bit touchy. And it wasn't just that I sometimes had problems understanding a dog's logic. No—it was the whole situation.

The Dogawandans had their philosophy about living in the Now in which case Tammy and Mark were both fine. But in my world, this was a tragedy. And what would Jimmy G say? Probably something like, "Hell's bells! There goes our meal ticket. We'll never get paid now!"

There were not enough rooms at the station for the sheriff to put us all into other rooms, so all the Dogawandans were lined up on the benches in the waiting room. Alice was directed to keep us all quiet, and she enforced this rule by glaring at us over the top of her cat-eye glasses. Even my talking to Pepe triggered a reproving look.

The sheriff, probably out of deference, had questioned Crystal first, and she swept out after only a few minutes. Artichoke and Terry were also in the first batch and dismissed rather quickly. Terry gave me a quick look of sympathy as she passed. Artichoke frowned when she saw me but did not stop to chastise me. Whatever punishment I was going to suffer for being "off leash" was being postponed.

I was the last person to be called into the sheriff's private office, and he seemed exhausted. He motioned me to a chair and sighed.

"So what do you know about this tragic incident?" he asked.

"I know quite a lot!" I said, eager to spill what I knew. I told him about finding the money orders and my visit to Broadbent and how I had last seen Mark storming into the city hall.

"And you think that had something to do with his suicide?" the sheriff asked.

"Not suicide," I said. "Obviously the man was murdered."

"What makes you think he was murdered?"

"Motive, means, and opportunity," said Pepe.

"Broadbent had a motive," I said. Though come to think of it, I couldn't think what it was. "Something to do with the money."

"Why would Tammy Darling be giving Barry Broadbent such a large sum of money?" asked the sheriff.

"Exactly!" I said. "And he had the means. All those guns in his office. I think you'll find the gun that killed Mark Darling was one of Broadbent's guns. Plus he had the opportunity. He was the last person to see Mark Darling."

"Except for our boss," said Pepe.

"Oh yes, except for our boss, Jimmy G. He was heading over there the last time we saw him."

"Which was?"

"I don't know exactly. Maybe about two p.m.," I said.

"So about an hour before Mark killed himself," the sheriff said.

"He didn't kill himself," I said. "Why would he?"

"I think it's obvious. After finding out about his wife and the councilman, he went up to the spot where she died and shot himself. Trying to join her in death, or something romantic like that."

"Mark was not the romantic type," I said.

"You seem to know him pretty well," the sheriff observed. He looked tired.

"It's just that he was always more concerned about money than his wife's happiness," I said.

"Or Fuzzy's," said Pepe.

"Oh my God, poor Fuzzy!"

"What?"

"Mark's dog! Or rather, Tammy's dog. She's in the impound."

"How did she get there?"

"I don't know. We noticed her when we went to get the wolves."

"Can we get her out, Geri?" Pepe asked.

"Can you get her out?" I asked the sheriff. "Write a note or something and say we're empowered to take care of her?"

"We?" The sheriff looked all around.

"Me and my dog," I said.

Pepe nodded.

The sheriff chuckled. "Sure!" He scribbled something on a piece of letterhead. I clutched it in my hand.

"So are you going to question Broadbent?" I asked.

"Yeah," said the sheriff. "Perhaps he will have

some insight into the guy's frame of mind. He might be able to tell us why the guy would go shoot himself. Got to talk to Frogeyes as well."

"Frogeyes?"

"Oh, that's what we all called James Gerrard at Fire Base."

"Ha!" said Pepe. "Now we know Jimmy G's Dogawandan name."

Chapter 36

Pepe and I went by the vet's office to see if we could get Fuzzy out of impound, but the front door was locked and a sign read CLOSED. We circled around back, through an alley. We could peer over a wooden fence and see into the kennel area. Fuzzy had been moved into one of the big cages where the wolf had been the day before. When she saw us, she began barking, rapid, high-pitched barks, while leaping into the air.

"Can you pick locks, Geri?" Pepe asked.

"No," I said.

"It is a skill you need to learn," said Pepe.

"It's not covered in *The Private Detective's Bible*," I explained.

"I will tell her we are coming back for her," said Pepe, edging closer to the fence. I couldn't tell how he communicated with the frantic dog, but she eventually stopped barking and settled down, her head between her paws.

"Did you tell her?" I asked. "About Mark?"

"She already knew," said Pepe.

"How?" I asked.

"We *perros* know these things," he said.

"Is she sad?"

"She is more upset about losing Tammy than Mark, but she is also very scared about what will become of her."

"I hope you told her—"

"That we will take care of her," said Pepe. "Of course. We cannot leave a good dog in prison."

"I thought you didn't like her," I said as we headed over to the Wagon Wheel to see if we could find Jimmy G.

"Her courage has most impressed me," said Pepe.

"Courage?"

"Searching for her mistress. She would have done anything to protect Tammy. That is how she got lost and ended up in the dog prison."

Unfortunately, we had missed Jimmy G. No answer when we knocked on the door of his room at the motel. I guess he was probably at the police station talking to the sheriff. So we headed over to the resort to find Felix. It was quite a contrast to the town and to the Dogawanda compound: an ultra-modern version of an old-fashioned lodge, five stories tall and sprawling, on the banks of the Cle Elum River. I parked my old Toyota at the far end of the vast parking lot, and Pepe and I trudged across to the entrance. The lobby was enormous, with huge windows that looked out over a stunning view of forest and mountains.

We took the elevator to the sixth floor and located room 602. I knocked. There was no answer. Felix could be out eating dinner. There was a restaurant off the lobby. What now? Felix had given me a room key. Should I just use it to let myself in? I had a momentary fantasy of slipping into his bed and surprising him when he returned.

Pepe seemed to be reading my mind. "Bad idea!" he said. "You should call him on your cell phone."

That was a good idea. Unfortunately, that wasn't any more effective. The call went straight to voice mail.

"Well, he gave me the key for a reason," I said to Pepe, "so I'm going to use it."

Pepe just shook his head.

It took me a few minutes to get the door open. I had to experiment to get the card facing the right way so it lit up the green lights and I could turn the knob. As soon as I got into the room, I could tell why Felix had not answered the knock or the cell phone. He was in the shower. I could hear the water running.

The room was beautiful. It occupied a corner of the hotel and had windows looking out over the forest on one side and the river on the other. The bed was rumpled—it looked like it had been slept in—and a white terrycloth bathrobe was lying across it.

Once again, my imagination leaped into action.

I contemplated shedding my clothes and sliding behind the shower curtain with a soapy Felix. Hmmmmm! Of course, we hadn't quite gotten to that stage in our relationship. But maybe it was time to start.

"No, Geri!" said Pepe, jumping up on me with his sharp little claws.

"How do you know what I'm thinking?" I asked.

"It is not thinking that you are doing," said Pepe. "You must know that we dogs are experts at reading body language. You are like a moth circling around a white flower at night."

"What? How do you know that?"

"The Nature Channel," said Pepe. "But there is an important distinction here. My keen sense of smell tells me that this is not the flower you want to fly into."

And at that moment, the door to the bathroom opened and Chloe walked out in a cloud of steam, a white towel wrapped around her body. She screamed and the towel fell off. Now she was naked, and shivering again.

"What are you doing here?" she screamed.

"Where's Felix?" I asked, looking behind her and thinking maybe they had been taking a shower together.

"What are *you* doing here?" she asked again. There was a pounding at the door.

"Are you OK in there?" It sounded like Felix.

"It is Felix," said Pepe.

I pulled open the door. There was a moment of

confusion as Felix took in the sight of the naked Chloe and then me, his eyes darting back and forth between the two of us.

"What's going on?" he asked.

"That's what I want to know!" I said.

"She busted into the room while I was taking a shower!" Chloe complained. She didn't seem uncomfortable being naked, just cold. She strolled over to the bed and pulled on the white terrycloth bathrobe that was lying on the rumpled coverlet.

"What is she doing in your room?" I asked Felix.

"This isn't my room," he said.

"Well, then, why did you give me the key to this room?" I asked. I showed him the key, which was still in my hand.

Felix looked horrified. "I guess I gave you the wrong one," he said.

"So you have a key to her room?" I asked.

"It's not like what you think," said Felix.

Chapter 37

"Ah, that is a great line," observed Pepe. "And it is always like what you think. At least in the telenovellas. Not so in a sitcom, however."

"Is this a sitcom? Or a telenovella?" I asked.

"What do you think, Geri?" asked Pepe. He seemed especially wise at that moment.

"Chloe thought there was bad energy in her room, so we switched rooms. We must have mixed up the keys," Felix said.

"Sounds more like a sitcom," I said, answering my own question.

"Or *A Midsummer Night's Dream*," said Pepe. I'm always a little bit surprised by his love for Shakespeare. You can't say that about too many dogs.

I looked at Chloe. Her eyes narrowed. "Something awful happened in that room! I just know it!" So it seemed to be true.

"Come on! I'll show you my room," Felix said.

"You can tell me what you think. I have to admit I don't think it's any different than this room."

Felix's room was right next door, which didn't actually allay my concerns. In fact, I noted that there was a communicating door between the two rooms, so presumably any bad energy could leak through to the other room, and presumably the two of them could visit each other late at night.

"Ah! Miss Chloe is right," said Pepe, trotting into Felix's room and beginning to sniff around the edges. "A big dog was here recently and left many evidences of his occupation." He began to lift his leg.

"Don't do that!" I said sharply.

"Very well," said Pepe, putting his leg back down. He continued sniffing, but this time the air. "Bad cologne. Old pizza. Cheap beer. I believe Chloe is correct. There is definitely an aura of unhappy male energy in this room. And it was not just the Rottweiler."

"How do you know it was a Rottweiler?" I asked.

Pepe shook his head. "How do you know a rose from a lilac?" he asked. "All flowers smell different. So do all dogs."

"What's going on?" asked Felix, who had been watching us.

"Pepe is telling me what he can smell in the room," I said.

Felix looked at me sideways.

"You mean, you're guessing by looking at his body language?" asked Felix cautiously.

I guess it was time for me to come clean with Felix. I had been trying to tell him the truth about Pepe for months. "No," I said. "I can actually hear what he's saying."

"But he's not saying anything," said Felix. He looked worried.

I sighed. "I know it's hard to believe, but I can hear him as clearly as I can hear you."

"More clearly," said Pepe to Felix, "since you are often concealing your true feelings behind your words."

"What true feelings?" I asked.

"I really care about you, Geri," said Felix, taking me into his arms. "And so if you tell me your dog speaks to you, I will have to believe you."

"You will? You do?" I asked. It seemed too easy. But looking into Felix's dark eyes, which were full of love, and feeling his arms around me, well, it made everything OK.

Felix drew me down to sit beside him on the wide double bed.

"Watch it!" said Pepe. "He is like the white flower and you are the moth."

"I have something I have to tell you," Felix said. He looked down at the ground as if searching for words on the carpet.

"It can't possibly be as weird as having a talking dog," I said with a nervous laugh. I still could hardly believe that I had finally told Felix my secret and that he seemed OK with it.

"I wish it was," said Felix. "It's really bad." He

winced. "It has to do with why I left L.A. and stopped working in the film business."

I was quiet. There was really nothing I could say.

Not so my dog. He said, "I am not weird."

"You see," said Felix, "the last time I worked with wolves, it didn't go so well." He sighed. "I was working with real wolves, not hybrids, on an adventure movie that was supposedly set in Alaska. But we were filming it on a sound stage in Burbank. Anyway, the female lead was Rita Knight—"

"Really?" She was one of my favorite actresses. But then she had a terrible accident and hadn't appeared in public since. A wild animal had mauled her during a film.

"You?" I turned to Felix, horror in my eyes. He misinterpreted my response and got up and walked away.

"Yes," he said, standing at the window and looking out at the dark woods. The sun glinted off the water of the river. "I was the trainer on that film. She was feeling so confident about the animals that she went to kiss one of the wolves on the snout and it bit her. Almost ripped off her chin." He shook his head. "She had to have reconstructive surgery, but she will never look the same."

"But that wasn't your fault!" I said, going up to stand beside him. I put my arms around him. He let me but did not respond.

"It was my fault!" he said. "I'm responsible for setting the standards so people on the set know what is safe and what is not. That's why it freaked me out so much when you did what you did today."

"So that's how you became an expert witness," I said.

"Well, yes," said Felix. "Rita sued the film company, and I had to explain that what the wolf did was instinctive. It didn't save the animal, though. He was killed. And the movie was never completed. The company went bankrupt trying to pay the legal fees."

"So that's why you left Los Angeles," I said.

"I wanted a new start," he said. "So I was really reluctant when Tavo tried to get me involved in this film. He thinks I should get back into the film industry. He thinks I need a challenge. I tried to tell him that you and your dog are enough of a challenge for me." He hugged me close. "I have enough on my mind, worrying about you being a private detective and getting mixed up in all these murders."

"It is good he does not know of the most recent one," said Pepe.

"I'm just not feeling comfortable about these hybrids," Felix went on. "I wish we could call off the shoot. But with everyone counting on me . . ."

"You've been doing great with them," I said. "You saved their lives. You would think they would know that."

"With a wild animal, you never know what it's thinking," said Felix.

"I can tell you what they are thinking," Pepe offered.

"Perhaps my dog can help," I suggested.

"Geri!" Felix tipped up my chin with his fingers. His eyes were shining. "You don't know what it means to me that you are always on my side."

"But you are always on my side—" I started to say, but he cut me off with a long, lingering kiss. Felix is a good kisser. No, rather, Felix is a great kisser. I get lost in his kisses. And that first kiss was followed by another, while we entangled our arms and legs around each other, and pretty soon, we were staggering toward the bed and then landing on it, all the while kissing and unbuttoning and moving against each other in ways that were breathtaking.

I worried for a moment about Pepe and what he might see as Felix helped me out of my Dogawandan shirt and then pulled off his own T-shirt, but I noticed he had disappeared from sight. Perhaps hiding under the bed? Or holed up in the bathroom?

I trusted he could take care of himself. It seemed like the moment I had been waiting for was finally arriving and Felix and I would be able to satisfy our desire for each other as we sprawled across the luxurious bed.

I sank back against the covers, shivering as I felt Felix's bare flesh against mine and then his lips on my breasts, licking and then blowing gently, a sensation that was driving me wild.

Then there was suddenly a cold breeze in the room and another shriek. It was Chloe, standing in the doorway between the rooms, still wearing only the bathrobe. To my surprise, Pepe was right by her side, and not growling.

"What is she doing here?" Chloe said to Felix, who sat up abruptly. I grabbed my shirt and clutched it to my bare chest.

"What are you doing?" he asked.

"I thought you were going to give me some lessons," she said.

"Yes, why don't you give her some lessons!" I said, pushing Felix aside.

"Wait, Geri! You don't understand," Felix said.

"How often can you use that line?" I asked, pulling on my shirt and grabbing my purse. "Come on, Pepe, let's get out of here."

I was furious and blinded by tears as I headed out of the room, with Pepe at my side. All the time I could hear Felix and Chloe arguing in the room.

A ping announced the arrival of the elevator, and as the doors swooshed closed, their voices were cut off. I was left alone with my own pain.

"Why did I trust him?" I said to Pepe.

"He made himself vulnerable to you," Pepe said. "Like falling on the ground and baring your throat."

Chapter 38

I'd been crying off and on as we drove back to the Dogawandan compound. I didn't want to cry in front of my dog, but I couldn't help it.

"You should take it like a dog," Pepe told me.

"Is that a variation of 'you should take it like a man'?" I asked him.

"*Sí*. In a way."

"Well," I told him, "I'm neither a man nor a dog. I'm a woman."

"Well, duh!" he said as if I'd just told him that grass was green or the sky was blue.

"So what did you mean by saying I should take it like a man? That I should just suck it up and act like I'm not hurt by Felix and Chloe?"

"That is one interpretation," he said. "But remember, I said take it like a *dog*."

"What's that supposed to mean?"

"Geri," Pepe told me, "in the *perro* world, we fight our rivals. That or roll over and let them walk all over us. You must decide whether to fight for Felix or roll over."

"What are you now, Dr. Phil?"

"You may think of me that way if you wish. Right now he would ask you, 'So, how's that workin' for you?'"

"Not well," I told him in all honesty.

"My point exactly," said Pepe. "You must remember that males and females are different."

It was my turn to say, "Well, duh!"

"By which I mean," Pepe continued, "the male *perro* is not subtle when he wishes to mate. He does not wine and dine. He goes straight to the female *perro*, gives her a sniff, and tries to do the deed. He is either rebuffed with a bark and a bite, or she makes herself available."

"Yes, Pepe, I know that."

"Ah," he said, before going on to discount my statement of the obvious. "But there is often a difference between what you know and what you *do*. You must remember this: when it comes to mating, it is always the female who makes the choice."

Now my dog sounded like a combination of Dr. Phil *and* Dogawanda. But I saw his point.

"Of course," said Pepe, gazing out the window. "Do not take my words of advice to mean that I approve of this match. I do not think he is worthy of you."

"You would not think any man was worthy of me," I said.

"That is untrue," he said.

"Name one man you would approve of," I said.

He thought about that for a minute, then said, "Ramon from *Paraiso Perdido*."

"But Ramon is a fictional character," I pointed out. "He's not real."

"Reality is just an illusion," Pepe said.

I just shook my head. "Dogawanda is really rubbing off on you," I said.

I was afraid I would run into Artichoke back at the ranch and be asked to explain my absence, but despite a brief encounter with a guard at the gate, I was able to slip into my room unnoticed. Completely worn out from all of the emotional turmoil of the day, I climbed into bed. Pepe jumped up and snuggled beside me and we both drifted off to sleep.

The next morning we decided over a quick breakfast that our first order of business was to go rescue Fuzzy. As we headed down Main Street, we passed a balding man wearing a shabby sports coat who seemed to be mumbling to himself. Pepe growled softly.

"That's rude, Pepe," I said. "That poor guy probably can't help himself."

"Yes, he can, Geri," said Pepe. "That's our boss! And he's not talking to himself—he's singing."

"You've got to be kidding!" I pulled over and waited until the man ambled up past my window. It was indeed Jimmy G. He was not wearing his fedora, which was why I had noticed his bald spot for the first time. And he was singing. It was a rather garbled version, but I thought I recognized an old Spikes hit: "Junkyard Dog."

I rolled down the window. "Hey, boss!" I said.

He turned around and looked at me, clearly puzzled. Then his expression cleared and a big grin spread across his face.

"Geri and her rat-dog!" he said. "Top of the morning to you!" He lifted his hand, apparently to tip his hat, then brought it down empty. He looked confused.

"You lost your fedora somewhere!" I said.

"Well, that's too bad, but Jimmy G has good news," he said. He reached into his pocket and brought out a handful of bills. "Moola! And oodles of it!"

"How did that happen?" I asked.

"Let Jimmy G take you and the rat-dog out to breakfast and I'll tell you all about it," he said.

That sounded OK with me—I could use a coffee—so we gave Jimmy G a ride to the diner, which was only a few blocks away.

"So where did all the money come from?" I asked my boss after the waitress took our order. Jimmy G had encouraged us to get anything we wanted. Pepe wanted an order of bacon, extra crispy. I went for a short stack of pancakes, since grains were forbidden on the Paleolithic diet. Jimmy G ordered the rancher's breakfast: a steak, two eggs over easy and some hash browns, plus two cups of coffee.

"Poker game," he said. "Jimmy G cleaned their clocks."

"Where did you find a poker game in this town?" I asked.

"Not in town," Jimmy G said. Our coffees arrived. He fished two ice cubes out of his water glass and plopped them in his cup. Then he swilled down the whole mug at once. Sitting across from him, I could smell the cigar smoke that saturated his clothes and the bourbon wafting out of his pores. "Indian casino, just a few miles away."

"How much did you win?" I asked.

"Enough to cover the back rent!" Jimmy G said. "Too bad about Mark, though. But this will set us straight." He blinked and chugged the second cup of coffee.

"Did you talk to the sheriff?"

"Yeah, Ray thinks the guy killed himself. He actually asked Barry if he could borrow one of his guns. Said he was going hunting."

"That's weird," I said. Mark didn't seem like the hunting type. "I would think he would be pissed at Broadbent. After all, his wife gave all of their money to him."

Our food arrived. I crumbled up the crispy bacon for Pepe. He launched into it with gusto.

"Seems like it was a misunderstanding. Jimmy G didn't get the details." Jimmy G poked the napkin into his collar, covering up his shirt and tie, and tackled his steak.

I slathered my pancakes with syrup and began cutting them up into wedges. "So how did you find this poker game?" I asked.

"Broadbent was the one who suggested it," Jimmy G said. He poked the yolks on his over-easy eggs and the yellow liquid spread in pools around his hash browns. "Said he couldn't drink in town. Was sort of unpopular because of the way he voted on some zoning thing. So we headed out to the casino. Found a poker game. Barry dropped out pretty quickly, though. Then it was just me and Curly."

"Curly?"

"Big palooka," said Jimmy G. "Rough-looking, midforties maybe, but polite. Sure had a lot of questions. But that was part of his game: keep Jimmy G's mind off *his* game. But that didn't work."

"What kind of questions?"

"He was looking for some stripper he knew ten years ago. Said she danced at a club up off Lake City Way in Seattle. Went by the name of Breezy."

My heart did a flip-flop. "Did he say why he was looking for her?"

"Said he lost touch with her. Wanted to reconnect. Had just heard she was in Fern Lake."

"Boss," I asked, "why was this guy asking you about her?" I knew Jimmy G didn't know about Terry's stint working as a stripper, or her ex-boyfriend or her stint in the witness protection grogram.

"Don't have a clue," the boss told me. "Just assumed

he was trying to distract Jimmy G." The waitress came over to refill his coffee cup. "Well, come to think of it, Curly did get real interested when he learned Jimmy G was a private detective."

"You told him that?"

"Why not? He said that was real exciting. Got even more excited when Jimmy G told him about his operatives who were undercover in a cult that had a compound up here in the mountains."

"You told him that?"

"Why not? He said that was real interesting. Said he'd shown this Breezy's photo around town and nobody had seen her, but maybe he'd check out this cult."

"Oh my Dog!" I was starting to pick up the Dogawandan lingo. "I can't believe you did that!"

"Why? What's wrong, doll?"

I filled him in quickly on my sister and her story.

"Wow!" said Jimmy G. "Sounds like this Curly might be looking for her. And not because he wants to catch up on old times."

"Yes, and if that's true, she's in danger! We've got to get back!"

Chapter 39

"Geri," said Pepe as we hustled to the car. "We must warn your sister, *sí*, but we cannot leave Fuzzy behind."

"You're right," I told him. "But we've got to hurry."

We were lucky. With the help of the letter from Sheriff Pager, we were able to convince the vet to release her. She seemed happy to see us, leaping into the air and turning in circles.

On the way back to the ranch, Fuzzy and Pepe snuggled together on the backseat. I could only hear Pepe's side of the conversation, but it sounded very comforting. Maybe my dog was becoming a spiritual guru.

Back at the ranch, I saw Felix's car in the parking lot, along with some trucks that I assumed had brought up the cameras and lights for the film crew. There was also a trailer, which probably served as a temporary dressing room.

"Where is the craft table?" Pepe asked. He knew his way around a movie set from our days working on *Dancing with Dogs*.

"I doubt they have a craft table," I said, "but we can always get some food from the kitchen. Is Fuzzy hungry?"

"Are you?" Pepe asked.

Apparently her answer was a vigorous yes, because Pepe reassured her. "Do not worry. They will not feed you grocery store kibble here."

When we crested the ridge where we had a view of the grounds, I saw the film crew set up in the meadow to our right, beside the yurt. But we headed straight for the lodge and ran right into Artichoke.

"Where have you been?" she asked.

I introduced her to Fuzzy and explained our mission of mercy. She turned up her nose at the sight of Fuzzy. Who could blame her? The poor dog was in even worse shape than when we had first seen her, her fur all dirty and matted and hanging over her eyes.

I asked her about Terry. Or rather Flicker. Or maybe Breezy.

"I haven't seen her today," Artichoke said. "But I've been looking everywhere for you. Crystal wants to see Pepe immediately. In the inner sanctum. She's preparing something fabulous for this evening, and she insists that he is part of it."

"OK, I'll take him up there," I said, heading for the stairs.

"Not you!" she said, stepping in front of me. "Your dog alone!"

"What about this dog?" I asked, pointing to Fuzzy. "Can she come along?"

"Fuzzy should come, too," Pepe said. "She might learn something from Dogawanda about being in the Now. She is still back in the past."

Artichoke shrugged. "I don't see why not."

I watched as Artichoke led them away. The two little dogs followed at her heels as she headed up the stairs. I have to admit I felt a little jealous.

But I had more important things to do. I needed to find my sister and warn her about the stranger who was looking for her. I wandered through the organic garden, visited the kitchen, took the path to the hot springs, looked into the lounge in the Beta Barn, but no one had seen her. Had she already packed up and left? Had the goon from Seattle found her? Several people suggested she might be watching the filming, so I headed over there.

The crew had set up in the big meadow to the east of the yurt. Tavo oriented me to the schedule for the day. They were filming some of the action shots with the wolves chasing Chloe, which they would later convert to look like night scenes. But they also wanted to film the rise of the full moon over the trees and pan down to the wolves running across the meadow.

Felix was at one end of the meadow, holding one

of the wolf-dogs. At a signal from the director, who was standing at the other end, he released it and the animal ran across the grass, so fast he was almost a gray blur. It was actually quite beautiful to watch: this magnificent animal in its prime, stretching out to his full capacity.

There were two cameras. One faced the meadow and the woods and could film the wolf-dog as it ran by. I was standing by the other camera, the one that Tavo was manning, along with the director and Chloe. It was set up so it would look like the wolf-dog was running straight at it. Very dramatic. Especially since the wolf-dog didn't stop. It was heading straight for us at full speed.

"Felix!" the director screamed. "Stop that wolf!"

"Will do!" Felix yelled back. He came running across the clearing after the wolf-dog.

My God, I thought. Were things going badly for Felix already? Chloe, who was standing near the director, wearing a flimsy pink dress, let out a shriek as the wolf-dog changed directions very slightly and seemed to home in on her.

That's when Felix got near enough to the beast to shout, "Stay!"

The wolf-dog hesitated, and Felix repeated the command with a sharp, downward motion of his right hand. "Stay!"

Amazingly, the wolf-dog obeyed. Felix went up, slipped him a treat of some kind, and then put a muzzle and leash on him.

"You've got to set that up better, bro," said Tavo.

"Yeah, I need to be at this end so he can hear the commands," said Felix. "I'll have to find someone else to let the hybrid go. If he knows the reward is over here, he should be good to go."

"Chloe, Rod, get over here. We need to shoot the kissing scene," said a woman with a clipboard. A guy got up from where he had been sitting under a tree on a folding chair. He wore only jeans; his chest was bare and he was ripped. Although those muscle men are not usually my type, I couldn't keep my eyes off of his abs.

Felix approached me. "Geri, I still want to explain."

"It's OK," I said. "I overreacted."

"Let me put this hybrid back in the pen," said Felix. "I'll be right back."

While he was gone, I stood on the sidelines watching as Chloe and the leading man were put into position in the tall grass of the clearing. As far as I could tell, he was supposed to have just morphed from a werewolf into a human and now he had her down on the ground and they were supposed to be kissing. Unfortunately, the scene was not going well. Chloe kept complaining that she was uncomfortable. There was a rock in her back. Rod's breath smelled bad. The camera was on her bad side. They took take after take.

"Chloe, for God's sake, do you think you could convince us that you actually enjoy kissing him?" the director was saying just as Felix came back to my side.

"Yes, why not kiss him like this," I said, deciding to kill two birds with one stone. I would be the one to show Chloe how to kiss—and I'd do it with Felix!

I took the startled Felix in my arms and kissed him right in front of everybody. And how I kissed him! I kissed him hard, I kissed him soft, I kissed him just caressing his lips with mine, and I kissed him deep and open-mouthed. There wasn't a type of kiss that I missed, never once coming up for air.

When we finished kissing, the director said, "Wow! That's the kiss I want! Thanks!"

Felix also smiled and said, "Wow! Me too!"

"Nice work, Geri!" said Pepe, bounding up to me with Fuzzy at his side. "I see you took my advice."

"I see you got Fuzzy," said Felix, remembering his last encounter with the little dog.

"Yes, after Mark died, the sheriff gave me permission to get her."

"Out of dog prison," said Pepe.

"She's a cute dog," said Felix, picking her up and scratching behind her floppy ears, "but she badly needs some grooming. Her hair is all matted and she hasn't had a bath in days. Can I take her back to the resort with me tonight and groom her?"

"If that's OK with her," I said, looking at Pepe.

"What do you think, Fuzzy?" Pepe asked.

Chapter 40

Apparently Fuzzy agreed because we left her in Felix's hands and headed back to the compound.

"So what did Star want?" I asked Pepe.

"She's going to hold some sort of special ceremony to announce a new training," said Pepe. "And she's going to feature me!" He seemed quite proud of himself. "She coached me a little on how to sit and where to put my attention. But she did not listen when I tried to tell her my ideas. I think, Geri, she can only hear me on the tape. Would that not be strange?"

"It would be strange," I agreed. "But I do think she was able to hear you during the last session. Remember how you told people to bark and then she told people to bark. And you said you were the moon goddess, and then she came up with the idea of the moon goddess."

"Maybe she can only hear me when she is in a trance," said Pepe.

"But that still means she can hear you," I pointed out.

"Not as well as you can," he said. "You can hear me all the time."

We had reached the front of the lodge. The lunch bell was ringing and the green-clad Dogawandans were filing into the dining hall. We headed inside and I looked around for my sister but did not see her at any of the tables.

Pepe insisted that he was hungry, so we went through the line.

"Geri, there is something I need to tell you," Pepe said after we settled down at a table in the back where I could see everyone as they entered. Pepe sat on the chair beside me, his eyes level with the tabletop. I had gotten a plate of roast beef for him and grabbed a nice ripe peach for myself. "Artichoke knows you are working for a PI."

"Really?" I almost dropped the peach I was biting into.

"Yes, she told Star that. She thought maybe you were looking for your sister."

"And how did Star react?" I set down the half-eaten peach.

"She was mad at Artichoke. She said it was Artichoke's responsibility to screen the participants." Pepe was so earnest he was ignoring the beef on the plate in front of him. Or maybe it was because it was too big for his mouth. I picked up a knife and began slicing it into small strips.

"So they didn't know we were looking for Tammy?"

"No, they did not make that connection. Instead Artichoke blamed your sister for that, too. She said that Flicker was responsible for the Darling fiasco."

"So they think my sister killed Tammy and Mark?" I asked.

"Star said she did not want to shelter a fugitive from the law. It might put them under scrutiny. She said they should turn her over to the police," said Pepe. He put his paws up on the table and sniffed the beef as I was cutting it.

"I wonder if Terry knows this," I said. "I wonder if she has already left."

"They also spoke about the money given to Broadbent. Star said she wanted nothing to do with it. Artichoke said it was necessary if Star insisted on expanding."

I put the knife down. Pepe started gobbling up the slices of beef, wolfing them down like he hadn't eaten in days.

I watched him for a minute. It was nice to see that our current situation did not affect his appetite. "Pepe, you should be able to smell my sister. Can you help me find her?"

It took a minute before he could respond, but then he said, "Of course, Geri. I thought you would never ask!"

He sat back on his haunches and closed his eyes. His whole little body began to shiver. He reminded me of somebody. It took a moment before

I realized who it was. He looked just like Star channeling Dogawanda.

"Close your eyes and look within," Pepe intoned in a deep voice. "And all will be revealed."

"Pepe, I don't need any of that phony wisdom!" I said.

"Do as I say!" he commanded. "You must obey your alpha!"

I sighed and closed my eyes. The next moment there was a pair of hands clapped over them, and a soft voice in my ear. "Surprise!"

It was my sister. She had slipped up behind me. What was even more surprising was that she was wearing my clothes: the jeans and embroidered Mexican top I had worn the first day. She had tied her hair back in a ponytail on the top of her head.

"I hope you don't mind," she said, sliding into the chair beside me. "I needed some normal clothes if I'm going to go out into the world again. And I knew your clothes would fit me!"

"Yes, back to old times!" I said. We had fought about this constantly as kids. She was always borrowing my stuff without my permission. "But I'm so glad to see you," I said, giving her a quick hug, "that I can't be mad at you."

"I just came to say good-bye," Terry said. "I'm leaving in a few hours. . . ."

"Terry, there's something I've got to tell you," I said. "There's a guy in Fern Lake who's looking for a stripper named Breezy."

Terry's face went pale. "That's the name I danced under."

"My boss met him at a casino. This guy said he had searched all over Fern Lake for her, but when he heard about the Dogawanda Center, he thought she might be hiding out up here."

"What does he look like?" Terry asked.

"Big guy, midforties, my boss said. He goes by the name of Curly."

"Oh my God! Curly. He's the enforcer for the mob!" Terry looked from right to left, as if scanning the crowd for him.

"Do not fear!" said Pepe, who had finished the beef and was licking the juice off the empty plate. "I have single-handedly brought down a Mexican drug cartel."

"What do you mean your boss?" Terry asked.

"My dog and I are private investigators," I said.

Terry started laughing. "You're kidding, right?"

"No," I said. "It's true. We work for a PI named Jimmy Gerrard."

Terry just shook her head. "So you're snooping around looking for clues."

"Yes, we're trying to figure out who killed Tammy," I said.

"Well, what have you learned?"

"I learned that you're in trouble," I said.

"I told you about that," she said. "It's all in the past."

"No, I'm talking about right now." As I spoke, Star and Artichoke entered the dining hall. I saw them looking in our direction. Star rang the large bell that hung at the front of the line. Instantly there was complete silence. The Dogawandans froze in their seats.

"I have an important announcement to make," Star said. "We will be gathering in the Longhouse for a very special session immediately after this meal. I expect everyone to attend." There was a murmur of assent and then the quiet murmur of conversation resumed but with an extra edge of excitement.

Star and Artichoke moved to the front of the line. They glanced our way before turning their attention to the items on the buffet.

"Do you know what she's talking about?" I asked my sister.

She shook her head.

I was worried. If Pepe was right, my sister might be the one in trouble. Or maybe me. What did the Dogawandans do to spies in their midst?

"Star and Artichoke were talking about turning you over to the police!"

"How do you know that?" Terry asked.

"She learned it from me!" Pepe said happily.

"My dog told me," I said.

Terry looked at Pepe and then she looked at me and then she looked at Pepe again.

"You know, I sort of believe you," she said.

"You do?" I hugged her again. "Nobody believes me when I say my dog talks!"

"What's family for," Terry asked, "but to believe in us when no one else will?"

"Ah! A most profound thought," said Pepe. And I realized that was true. I had to believe that Terry was innocent, just as she believed my dog could talk.

"Hey! I've got to get out of here!" said Terry, looking up and seeing that Star and Artichoke were approaching our table, their trays full of food. "Fox is going to give me a ride down to the bus station. I'll make him wait until I get on the bus safely. See you later, alligator." My eyes filled with tears at that familiar phrase. As kids, we could go on for hours with buttercups and humming birds. Terry gave me a quick kiss on the cheek and hurried out the side door.

"Where is she going?" asked Star with a frown as she set her tray down on the table.

"I don't know," I said. It was the truth. Star seemed satisfied by that.

"I am so excited about our meeting tonight," she said. Her eyes brightened as she looked at Pepe. "Now that Max has retired, we are so fortunate that you brought us this fantastic creature who serves as a mouthpiece for the Aztec moon goddess. I think we will all be surprised to hear what the moon goddess has to say."

Chapter 41

"Dearly beloved," said Star, spreading her arms wide so that the kimono gave her the appearance of a magnificent peacock, all shimmering turquoise and green. We were all gathered in the Longhouse. I was asked to sit on one of the pillows in the front row, along with Artichoke and Fox. "We have just received the news of a great victory. The city council approved our request for rezoning last night at the special hearing! We can begin building our new temple, which will be able to hold twice as many worshippers."

There was a burst of howling from the Dogawandans.

"Yes, it is truly an achievement. We have brought down our enemies through the power of positive reinforcement and mental telekinesis, transporting to them the vision of the great center we are establishing here on our land, which is now zoned for our expansion."

Another great howl echoed in the shadowy spaces at the top of the Longhouse.

"And now we must listen to the words of wisdom that flow to us from the Aztec moon goddess, Ixoli-Pixoli, who speaks to us through this magnificent creature." She gestured to Pepe, who was balancing precariously on a pile of pillows at her side, a pile of pillows that brought him almost level with her shoulders.

"Magnificent is right," said Pepe. "Moon goddess, not so much."

"Let us await the word of the Dog," said Star, bowing her head.

Star remained slumped over. Pepe looked at me, his eyes sparkling in the candlelight.

"Oh, wise people of Dogawanda," said Pepe, sitting up straighter. He surveyed the crowd before him with his bright eyes.

"Oh wise ones, beloved by Dogawanda," said Star, raising her head.

"But I am not Dogawanda," said Pepe.

"No, we are not speaking to Dogawanda today," said Star, "but to the moon goddess, Ixoli-Pixoli, who has come to share her visions for the future."

"I am not the moon goddess," said Pepe. "Do I look like a moon goddess?"

"See how his fur shines with the reflected radiance of tonight's full moon!" said Star. And it was true. Pepe's fur seemed to glow. The assembled crowd gasped. What was it? A trick of the light? Or did Pepe have magical powers?

"I come to you with the wisdom of the centuries behind me," said Pepe, seeming to settle into his role as the moon goddess.

"She brings us the wisdom of centuries," said Star.

"For centuries, we little dogs have wandered the earth, invisible to many, ignored by some, mistaken as mere lap dogs. . . ."

"She says . . . ," Star faltered. "I have," she began again, "been roaming the earth, ignored and misunderstood for centuries. . . ."

"Yet our small stature and amazingly cute appearance have worked in our favor."

"I may seem small but I am brilliant in appearance." That was Star's translation.

"We can go many places and gather information that others would prefer remain secret."

"I bring you the secret wisdom that has been long concealed."

"For instance," said Pepe, scratching his side, "do you know that when people scratch themselves, it becomes contagious. Others begin scratching, too."

Star looked puzzled but translated that as "Many small actions have ripple effects."

I looked around. Sure enough, here and there in the audience, I saw Dogawandans scratching themselves. A woman scratched her nose. A man ran his fingernails along the nape of his neck.

"And do you know why?" Pepe asked.

"Why?" Star asked, completely forgetting her persona.

"Scientists have determined there is an area of the brain called the scratch matrix from which such impulses are generated," Pepe intoned.

I have to say it is marvelous what my dog has learned watching TV.

Star took a moment to come up with a summary but eventually she said, "The human mind is a marvelous instrument."

"And," Pepe went on, "I also know that Mark Darling was murdered."

Star blinked. "I know the secrets of life and death," she said.

"And I know who murdered him."

"You do?" That was me.

"You do?" That was Star. She recovered quickly. "Yes, I know many things."

"I know," said Pepe, "that this same person was responsible for the murder of Tammy Darling.

"I also know that you bribed Councilman Broadbent with money you borrowed from Leaf so that he would vote in your favor during the hearing."

Star's eyes flew open.

"Did you not notice that I was there in the room while you talked with your minion? I can testify against you."

"You cannot testify against us," Star said, completely forgetting where she was. "You're nothing but a dog!"

"Nothing but a dog!" Pepe was indignant. So were the Dogawandans. Rustling and outcries.

Star turned to them. "I'm sorry," she said, holding out her hands. "The connection is fading. I'm unable to continue." She slumped forward dramatically.

"So much for appreciating the wisdom of dogs!" said Pepe.

Chapter 42

Pepe was shivering as we headed up the hill toward the clearing where the film crew was working. I wasn't sure whether he was shivering because of the cold—once the sun went down, the temperature had plummeted—or because he was stressed by the session with Star.

"Do you know who killed Mark?" I asked him.

"Not really," he said. "But I thought we might get someone to confess. Unfortunately, Star is an imperfect medium. She did not convey my exact words."

The session had ended in chaos. Fox had helped Star off the dais and out of the Longhouse. Artichoke had glared at me and told me to meet her in the Beta Barn for some discipline. I figured it was better to leave. I was hoping to hitch a ride back to the resort with Felix and the film crew and come back for our stuff in the morning. That way I might get another chance to spend time with my sister. Plus spend the night with Felix.

When we arrived at the meadow, it looked much different from earlier in the day. A few lights were set up, down low among the trees. They cast eerie shadows on the tree trunks. But the full moon was so bright there was almost no need for lights. It had just risen over the tree line and illuminated the entire scene.

The cameras were still in the same positions, one on the side, the other at the end. The director and actors huddled around the camera in the woods. Felix and the wolf-dogs were nowhere in sight. Chloe was shivering as usual, perhaps because she was clad only in a fluttery pink chiffon dress, but someone had loaned her a black Windbreaker. She wore it draped over her shoulders.

"Chloe, I keep telling you, you don't have to worry about the wolves," the director said. "They won't be out there at the same time you are."

"Where are they now?" asked Chloe, looking up and down the meadow, still nervous.

"Felix has them restrained over there," said the director. He pointed to the other end of the meadow. "We're going to shoot the wolves first." He spoke Felix's name into a mike pinned to his lapel.

I saw Felix step out into the moonlight from the shadows of the trees and wave his hands.

"We're ready for the shot with the wolves," the director said.

Felix turned around to speak to someone behind

him, then headed over to our end of the set at a
brisk run. He gave me a quick hug when he saw me,
then signaled his assistant in the shadow of the
trees. I could see the two wolf-dogs, low gray shapes
standing by the person in the distance. The director gave instructions to both cameramen. Chloe
stood to one side, hugging herself.

At a signal, the wolf-dogs were released and came
streaking across the clearing. They looked magnificent in the moonlight, just like wild wolves, sleek
and graceful, bounding through the grass. As they
got closer to us, Chloe shrieked and covered her
eyes, turning her back. The wolf-dogs came on,
closer and closer.

"Stay!" Felix's command rang out, and the wolf-
dogs skidded to a halt. They lay down in front of
him. It was quite amazing. I almost hugged him.

"Great work!" said the director. He checked in
with the two cameramen and they both said they
wanted a second take.

"Nice work, cousins," said Pepe to the wolf-dogs.

"Can we do my scene next?" Chloe asked.

"Sure!" The director looked around. "Just remember. In this scene, we're going to superimpose
the shot we just took of the wolves running. So
when I call action, run toward us. Look at the
camera, then look behind you and pretend you see
the wolves chasing you. Look at the camera again
and scream. Run even faster and as you approach
the mark, fall down. That will be the point at which
the werewolf overtakes you and changes into a

man. We shot that earlier. Think you can handle that?"

Chloe nodded.

"Why don't you go hang out with Tavo at the other camera?" Felix said to me. "I'm going to walk the hybrids back so they're in position for the next round."

I headed over to the camera to the side of the set. Chloe passed by us, trudging through the tall grass, until the director called out that she should stop. We all waited as everyone got into position. Felix delivered the animals to his assistant and then walked back and stood beside me and Pepe, putting his arm around my shoulders.

Chloe shrugged off the Windbreaker and tossed it into the woods.

"Action!" screamed the director.

Chloe began running.

She looked so vulnerable, with the pink dress fluttering around her, the dark trees in the background. I could see why they had chosen her for this part. She truly looked like a victim. But she did not look scared. She was supposed to be screaming, but she was simply uttering little halfhearted shrieks as she ran and looking back over her shoulder with the bored expression of someone maybe playing hide-and-go-seek.

"Look terrified!" the director shouted.

"She is a terrible actress," said Pepe.

Just as she passed us, Chloe looked back over her shoulder and suddenly she did indeed look terrified.

"Wow! She takes direction well," said Pepe.

But it wasn't the direction that was motivating her. As I looked to the right, I saw the wolf-dogs bounding out of the woods behind her, snarling and snapping. Chloe screamed and ran like her life depended on it.

"My God!" I said.

"This is not good," said Pepe.

"What the hell!" Felix ran forward. "Chloe, stop running!" he yelled.

Chloe screamed, then tripped and fell down—just like the director had told her to do. Except this was for real.

"Keep the camera rolling!" the director yelled. "This is great footage!"

Felix had almost reached Chloe's side. But so had the wolf-dogs.

Chloe scrambled to her feet just as Felix reached her.

"Stop!" Felix commanded the wolf-dogs, getting between them and her. "Stay, damn it!"

Chloe ran right past him, heading into the woods, and soon was gone from sight, though we could hear her crashing through the underbrush and screaming as she went.

My heart was in my throat as Felix confronted the wolf-dogs. They veered around him and took off into the woods, heading after Chloe. Felix ran after them.

"You are safe now," Pepe told me. "I must go help Felix. He needs help."

He was gone, too, before I could object.

What a disaster. I couldn't let my dog go after Felix and those wolf-dogs alone. But then I heard a voice shouting, "Over here!"

It was Artichoke. She had come out of the woods to my right. Her long braid had come loose and was flapping around her shoulders. She seemed frantic.

"Help me!" she said. "We've got to get their leashes and muzzles so they can be restrained."

I followed her to the other end of the clearing. I could no longer hear the sounds of the chase, but I could see her point. Felix could not simply wrestle the wolf-dogs to the ground. I wondered what had gone wrong with his assistant.

We emerged in a clearing, and I saw two large wire cages that had been set up to confine the wolf-dogs until they were needed. Two chain leashes were staked to the ground, and attached to the ends of them were the wide leather collars for the animals. "Where's the assistant?" I asked. "How did they get out of their collars?"

"I don't know," said Artichoke as she bent over one of the leashes and unhitched it from the stake to which it had been fastened. "Hurry!"

I bent down and unhooked the other leash.

"This way!" said Artichoke, heading into the woods.

Chapter 43

We headed off at an angle that might intersect with the wolf-dogs. But I could no longer hear any sounds of the chase or calls for help. Artichoke trotted ahead of me, her braid swinging as she ran, the leash dangling from her hand. I followed behind, heading deeper into the woods.

The moonlight cast a strange blue light over everything.

Suddenly Artichoke stopped.

"Listen!" she said. "I think I hear them!"

I stopped too. But I didn't hear a thing.

Suddenly Artichoke advanced on me, the leash clenched in both hands. Her eyes glittered in the moonlight. Like the eyes of the wolf-dogs.

"What do you think you're doing?" I asked.

She took a step forward, the chain-link leash glinting in the moonlight. "Taking care of a bad dog," she said, continuing to come toward me.

I backed away from her. It seemed clear that I was the "bad dog."

"You can't get away with this," I said. "Help! Pepe!" I shouted.

"Your precious dog won't help you now," she said, continuing to advance on me.

"Felix!" I yelled as I backed up, my feet slipping slightly on the uneven ground.

"He can't help you either," she said, snapping the chain taut between her hands. "They're both too busy with the wolves."

Then I saw her face change. "I guess I was wrong."

I turned around, expecting to see Pepe or Felix behind me. But there was nothing there. Just an empty path in the moonlight. The next moment, with a loud "Ha!" Artichoke had looped the chain around my neck and was pulling. I lashed out with the chain I held, but although I could feel it making contact with her, it didn't stop her. She was slowly cutting off my air supply.

Just as I felt the world turning to black around me, I remembered a trick from a self-defense class I once took where the instructor told us the best strategy is to move in the opposite direction from what the attacker expected. I slumped forward against the chain and ducked my whole body forward. That shift of weight threw her off balance and she loosened her grip. I was able to back up and slip out from the leash.

I took off running. I tried to call out, but when I

tried to shout, it came out in a croak rather than a scream or a cry. I headed in the direction of the meadow, thinking I would be safe. Artichoke wouldn't dare attack me in front of the film crew.

But somehow I got turned around. Instead of the meadow, I saw only endless trees before me. I zigzagged back and forth, looking for something familiar, all the time hearing footsteps and brush crackling behind me. Artichoke was silent, but I knew she was deadly and I knew she was able to track me because of the noise I was making.

I began moving more slowly and deliberately, trying to imitate the silent pad of the wolf-dogs, and, in turn, the sound of pursuit diminished. Perhaps Artichoke was stopping, listening. The full moon shone down through the trees. It was almost as bright as a city street. There was no place for me to hide. I couldn't see her, but that didn't mean she wasn't out there watching me, perhaps from the shadow of a taller tree.

To my left, I spotted the pen of the wolf-dogs. I must have gone really far because the pen was on the far side of the property. But this was good. It meant I was close to the lodge and the other buildings. Which meant I was pretty close to safety.

That's what I thought. Until Artichoke came rushing at me out of the woods, waving the chain. I headed for the only place that seemed to offer safety: the open door to the pen. I thought I could slam the door behind me and the chain-link fence would protect me from Artichoke's assault, but she was quick. She tugged on the gate as I struggled to hold it closed.

"You've been a bad dog," she hissed. "You need to be punished!"

I dug in my heels. Used all my strength to hold the door shut, my fingers clamped over the wires of the chain link.

Artichoke looked gleeful. She slashed at the fence with her metal chain, lacerating my fingers.

"Ow!" I screamed, and let go. Big mistake.

Artichoke saw her opportunity and flung herself at the gate. It swung open and I scrambled toward the back of the pen, contemplating my options. Climb the fence? Cower in the enclosure? Use the metal water bowl as a shield?

"Thought you could outsmart me, did you?" Artichoke asked. "You and your stupid purse dog are no match for me and Dogawanda."

I backed up as she advanced, swinging the metal leash.

If I had been a dog, I would have laid down, rolled over on my back, and presented my belly as a sign of submission. And if Artichoke had been a dog, she would have given a satisfied woof, her dominance established, and that would have been the end of that. But we weren't dogs. She was going to kill me.

Out in the woods, I heard the howling of the wolf-dogs. What was going on out there? I almost wished they were in the pen with me. I probably would stand a better chance against them than the beast that Artichoke had become.

Chapter 44

Artichoke was smiling as she advanced, a sinister smile. "You've been very, very bad," she said.

I decided to distract her with conversation, while my brain worked out ways to get around her.

"You are wrong!" I said assertively, trying to sound like a top dog.

"Oh, but I'm not!" she said. "You've been sniffing around where you're not wanted. You think I don't know what you do?"

"That's right. I don't think you know what I do," I said. Unfortunately, my assertive tone was not matched by my behavior. Artichoke was backing me up, step by step, toward the end of the pen.

"You're a private investigator," Artichoke said. "I can't believe I didn't know that until yesterday."

"Yes, you failed to do your research," I said. The gate was open at the other end of the pen, some sixty feet away. How could I get there and make my escape?

"And you're Flicker's sister," she said. "I should have known that, too."

"How did you find that out?" I was genuinely puzzled.

"She told me! She was proud your disgusting little dog was Crystal's new favorite!"

"He is not disgusting!" I stopped, outraged. Artichoke stopped as well, frowning at me.

"Max was a champion. Max was all we needed. That dog was the smartest, sweetest beast I've ever known. And now your little purse dog is going to represent the great Dogawanda. Ridiculous."

"So you're angry at me because of my dog?"

"No one takes Max's place!"

"So it's not because you murdered Tammy?"

"Well, yes, I murdered Tammy, but that bitch was going to ruin our plans. She was demanding her money back."

"What about Mark?" I asked. So far, so good. This was just like one of those crime shows on TV where the villains are so sure of themselves that they tell the hero everything about how they did the crime and why, thus giving the hero time to make a plan and save the day. Problem was, I didn't have a plan.

"He started snooping, too. Demanded his money back."

"How did you find that out?"

"Barry called me. Told me the guy was kicking up a fuss and to take care of it. Otherwise Barry wasn't going to throw us his vote. So I drove down there, picked Mark up, told me I'd give him his money back if he came with me to the ranch. It was easy! That one is highly motivated by money."

"Was."

"Is, was. Big deal. He's out of the picture and we got the rezoning approved."

"Not when I tell the sheriff about the bribe." I taunted her deliberately.

My plan was to make her so mad that she would rush at me and I would dart around her and make my escape. Fortunately, the first part worked. She flung herself at me. Unfortunately, the second part didn't work. I couldn't get around her. Instead she pinned me to the fence and pressed the metal chain against my neck.

I struggled, calling out for help, but my voice was just a tiny squeak. I had wasted my time talking to Artichoke when I should have been screaming my lungs out. This was the time in a TV show when the police would bust onto the scene with their guns drawn.

That didn't happen.

Chapter 45

But something even better did. There was a crashing sound in the underbrush and the wolf-dogs came loping into the clearing, heading straight into the pen. They didn't stop until they were a few yards from me and Artichoke. They were both breathing heavily, their mouths open and saliva dripping from their sharp fangs.

Artichoke gasped and stepped aside, trying to sidle along the fence toward the open door. I remained quiet and still. Felix had taught me that any quick movements or sudden cries might trigger their prey instinct. But Artichoke didn't know that.

She shrieked. She slashed at them with the chain. She whirled around and around. That seemed to make them angry. They didn't even look at me. They began to circle her.

"Help me!" she cried.

Fat chance, I thought. But I really didn't want to see the wolf-dogs tear her into shreds. What to do?

Also I was afraid to leave, as the wolf-dogs were between me and the gate.

I heard rustling in the underbrush and Pepe appeared. My tiny white savior! He didn't hesitate but ran into the pen and positioned himself between me and the wolf-dogs.

"*Hola*, brothers," he told the wolf-dogs. "You do not want to harm my partner, Geri. She is a friend to all canines."

"Pepe, she was trying to kill me!" I said, pointing at Artichoke. "She's the one who killed Tammy and Mark."

Pepe growled and began circling Artichoke, along with the wolves. "But this one you may have for a plaything," he said.

More crashing in the underbrush. Felix appeared. He was breathing heavily, too, but he understood the seriousness of what he saw immediately. He rushed into the pen and gathered me into his arms.

"What's going on, Geri?" he asked.

"Artichoke tried to kill me," I said. "She's a murderer." I could barely speak. I was shaking from fear and adrenaline.

"It's OK," he said. "Let's get you out of here." He turned to the wolf-dogs. "Pin her!" he said. The bigger of the two wolf-dogs jumped up on Artichoke and knocked her down. The other wolf-dog stood over her face, growling, his spit dripping on her nose. She was as white as a sheet and shivering like a Chihuahua. Meanwhile Pepe jumped on her prone body, saying, "Do not move a muscle or I will bite your nose off!" He positioned his tiny teeth right at her neck.

"Don't let them bite me!" she said through chattering teeth.

"I don't know if I can control them," said Felix, but it was clear he could, for when the wolf-dogs tried to back away, he told them to stay.

"You're safe now," Felix said, gently guiding me toward the gate. But he was wrong. Just as I was about to exit the pen, there was more rustling in the underbrush and Fuzzy appeared.

"Not much left for you to do," I said to her. But I was wrong.

Right behind her was a heavy-set, dark-haired guy. He looked really out of place in the woods, with his hands jammed in the pockets of his black leather sports coat.

"Who are you?" I asked.

"Curly," he said. "And you must be Breezy."

"Breezy? Not me. I'm Geri."

"Geri, Terry, what's the difference?" he said. "You look just like your photo."

"You've got the wrong sister, mister," said Pepe.

"Yes, you've got the wrong sister," said Felix.

"This is the end of the line for you, Breezy!" the guy said. He pulled his right hand out of his pocket and I saw he held a gun, which was aimed at my chest.

Felix rushed over and got in front of me. Pepe

jumped off Artichoke and came tearing out of the pen. But Fuzzy was even faster. She leaped into the air and chomped down on Curly's wrist. His shot went wild, crashing into one of the metal poles of the pen and ricocheting back, hitting him in the foot. He dropped his gun.

"Owww!" he screamed, hopping around on one foot. Fuzzy stayed attached to his wrist. Meanwhile Pepe darted in from behind and sunk his teeth into the Achilles tendon of his standing foot.

"What's going on? Why is he trying to shoot you?" Felix asked.

"It's a long story," I said. I dashed over and picked up the gun.

Curly was trying to shake off the two dogs. Fuzzy was still attached to his wrist, and he was slamming her against the chain-link fence. Pepe was clamped on his ankle, and he tried to kick him with his bleeding foot.

"Stop!" I commanded. "If you hurt those dogs, I'll shoot you in the other foot!"

We heard a rustling in the pen. Now that Pepe's little teeth were not at her throat, Artichoke was trying to rise. Felix turned around to give the wolf-dogs another command. "Hold!" he shouted, holding out his hand. Artichoke froze. The wolf-dogs froze, too, their eyes fixed on her.

I turned around in time to see Curly pulling a small pistol from inside his coat. He aimed it at Pepe. It seemed likely he would just shoot himself in the other foot, but I couldn't really take the chance that his aim would be bad again, because if he missed, he might hit my dog. I raised the gun in my hand but hesitated. I'd never shot anyone before.

Out of nowhere, Jimmy G appeared, running full tilt at Curly. The guy never saw him coming. He got tackled like a running back blindsided in a pro football game. His little pistol went flying, and he let out a big "ooof!" when he hit the ground. Luckily both Fuzzy and Pepe leaped aside as he fell. Jimmy G sat on top of him and gave him a couple of knocks on the head. I picked up the other pistol.

"Where did you come from?" I asked my boss.

Jimmy G stood up, dusted himself off, and said, "Jimmy G's always around when you need him, doll. You know that."

Applause erupted from the edge of the woods.

I looked around and saw that we had an audience: Tavo and Chloe and the director and a bunch of Dogawandans.

"Best footage I ever got!" Tavo said.

"You filmed this?" I asked.

"Yep!" He nodded.

"Magnificent acting!" said the director. "And some dynamite stunt work." He nodded at Jimmy G, who stood up and took a bow.

* * *

Eventually the police were called and Artichoke and Curly were led away in handcuffs.

"You know if it wasn't for you and Pepe," I said to Felix, "I wouldn't be alive."

"That is true," said Pepe.

"You know what, Geri?" said Felix. "For a minute, I thought I heard your dog talking." He shook his head. "But I guess it was just the stress of the moment. Anyway, he definitely helped save the day."

Pepe was insulted. "Helped?" he said sarcastically. "I was the white knight of a dog who galloped in and saved the day! *Arriba!*"

Felix looked bewildered. "Did your dog just say *Arriba?*" he asked me.

I smiled. "Yes, he did."

"There is hope for you yet, *amigo*," Pepe told him.

"I think we all need to get cleaned up," I said. Fuzzy's hair was matted with leaves and her muzzle spotted with Curly's blood. Pepe looked like he had been rolling around in the dirt. And I was drenched with sweat after my close encounter with Artichoke.

"Yes," said Felix, shaking off his momentary confusion. "We can arrange that." His brown eyes were warm. "Come back to the hotel with me. We can take a nice, long shower together."

"Hmmmmm," I said, leaning into him. "That sounds good."

"Me too!" said Pepe.

"Me too!" said Fuzzy.

Felix acted like he heard both dogs this time. But he didn't let it bother him.

"Of course," he said.

I wrapped my arms around Felix's waist and told him, "Might get a little crowded."

Chapter 46

The Private Detective's Bible advises you to write up case notes as soon as you close a case, so I sat down the next week and tried to summarize what Pepe and I were already calling the Dogawanda Case.

It seemed clear that from a financial point of view, the case was a disaster. With our client dead, we had no chance of getting compensated for our hours of investigating. If it hadn't been for Jimmy G winning all that money playing poker, we'd probably be getting evicted from our PI office in short order. The money he won would also cover my next paycheck, but I was still out the $5,000 I had paid for the next level of training. Star refused to return it to me, although she did offer to let me complete the training. I wasn't eager to return to the Dogawanda ranch and declined.

Because of the evidence that the Dogawandans had bribed Councilman Broadbent, charges were filed against him and the results of the hearing on the rezoning were overturned. So the construction site that had been the focus of two deaths was turned into the site of a memorial instead. Star claimed she had no knowledge of the bribe and that Artichoke had acted on her own, without Star's approval.

Artichoke disputed this, but since Pepe was the only witness who could provide any evidence that Star had known about the bribe, Star was off the hook. Artichoke was jailed and charged with bribery, assault with intent to commit murder, and two murders.

We never saw Terry again. Apparently she had left the Center with Fox and boarded a Greyhound bus while Curly was driving up to the ranch looking for her. For a while, I thought she might hear the news that Curly was in jail and come back home. But we haven't heard from her yet. Cheryl is mad at me for "losing" my sister after finding her. What can you do? She wasn't happy when Terry was found. And she wasn't happy when Terry was lost.

Max came out of retirement to channel Doga-wanda and the wisdom of Ixoli-Pixoli vanished, though Pepe from time to time suggested that we should hold our own channeling sessions. I refused.

Meanwhile, Felix had been charmed by the moxie shown by the little dog Fuzzy, and he adopted her. Felix brought her over frequently to show off how she was responding to his training. She could sit, lie down, roll over, shake paws, and stay on command, plus she trotted right by his side when we went for walks.

Pepe was not impressed. "She might be a good follower," he said, "but I am the Big Chihuahua."

Signed yours truly,
Dances-with-Dogs (yes, I finally got my Dogawandan name!)

Acknowledgments

Writing about a cult always sounds like a promising idea (both Waverly and Curt have tried this separately in separate unpublished novels) but it's not easy to strike the right balance between the humor that a cozy requires and the bizarre beliefs that characterize cults. We liked the idea of a cult that worshipped a dog, and from there we came up with the idea that they used (and misunderstood) dog training techniques as a method of shaping human behavior. At the same time, we wanted to highlight the plight of wolf-dogs, hybrids that are often euthanized when they become mature and display unacceptable levels of aggression. Waverly is especially grateful to Ceiridwen Terrill's memoir, *Part Wild: One Woman's Journey with a Creature Caught Between the World of Wolves and Dogs* for a story about the heartbreak involved in loving and raising a wolf-dog hybrid. We also gleaned information from Mission: Wolf, a sanctuary in southern Colorado for captive and former pet-wolves. Any mistakes are ours, and are based on common misconceptions about wolves, to which we have also fallen prey.

We need a team to help us write, publish and promote our novels. On the writing side, we are grateful for the support of our writing group (Linda Anderson, Rachel Bukey and Janis Wildy) though they didn't get a chance to give us feedback on this novel as we were writing too fast to share it at our biweekly meetings. Faizel Khan provides us with coffee and tuna sandwiches every Tuesday afternoon when we brainstorm at Café Argento. And the staff at Elliott Bay Cafe serve us coffee and morning sandwiches on Friday mornings.

On the publishing side, we are happy to have as part of Team Pepe: at Fine Print Literary, the enthusiastic support of our agent Stephany Evans with help from Becky Vinter and Heather Evans; at Kensington Books, the fine suggestions of our editor, Michaela Hamilton, with marketing support from Adeola Saul and excellent copy-editing from Carrie Andrews.

Promotion is also a team activity. We are grateful to the many marvelous members of Seattle's Sisters in Crime. Bharti Khirchner invited us to present on a panel at Northwest Bookfest and Judy Cobb Dailey arranged for us to be on a panel at the Pacific Northwest Writers Association conference. We had a great time at Bouchercon hanging out with another writing duo, Sparkle Abbey, whose constant presence at book and pet-related events we track on Facebook.

We are also grateful to all librarians, like Chapple Langemack, who arranged for us to talk at the branch of the Kitsap Regional Library, and all booksellers, but especially Karen Maeda Allman at Elliott Bay Book Company, Wendy Manning at Third Place Books, Christina Claassen at Village Books, and J.B at Seattle Mystery Book Shop.

And finally we rely on the editorial suggestions of our first reader and Pepe wrangler, Shaw Fitzgerald, the patience of Curt's wife, Stephanie Colbert (aka The Saint) and the inspiring presence of the little white Chihuahua who started it all: Pepe Fitzgerald.

In case you missed the debut adventures
of Geri and Pepe,
here is an excerpt from
the first Barking Detective Mystery . . .

DIAL C FOR CHIHUAHUA

Available from Kensington!

Keep reading for a sample . . .

Chapter 1

Apparently the fad was over. All those actresses and models who thought a miniature dog stuffed into a Versace shoulder bag was so cute were now abandoning their furry "accessories" in record numbers. The Los Angeles shelters were so full of Chihuahuas they had to fly them to other parts of the country. My new pet was one of forty Chihuahuas who had been shipped to Seattle.

At the Humane Society, the Chihuahuas were all in one cage. Most were milling around or throwing themselves at the bars, barking. One dog sat by himself, away from the others. A ray of sunlight fell through the opening high in the cinder block wall and illuminated his white fur.

I knew as soon as I looked into his big, dark eyes that he was mine. He held his head high but he looked forlorn. It was a feeling I could totally understand.

My divorce had just become final. My ex had already bought a new three-bedroom house with his fiancée, while I was scraping by in a one-bedroom condo with his cat. To make things worse, the real estate market was crashing, and my career as a stager was in jeopardy. After suffering through a series of disastrous dates, I decided to adopt a dog. I was in need of some unconditional love.

My new pet was quiet during the drive home but he turned into a little white tornado when I set him down on the carpet inside my front door. He raced around the living room, sniffing around the edges of the furniture. Luckily I had locked Albert, the cat, into my bedroom before I went to pick up my new companion.

While he was exploring, I went into the kitchen to set up a water bowl and food dish for him. I opened a small can of Alpo Gourmet, hoping he'd like beef and vegetables with gravy. At the snick of the can opener, he scampered around the corner, his nails clicking across the tile floor, before I could even spoon the food into his dish.

Poor little guy, I thought, he must be terribly

hungry. But instead of wolfing down the Alpo, he paused in front of his dish and just stared at it.

Maybe he didn't like beef and gravy. Maybe he didn't like vegetables. But I'd been in a hurry to get to the Humane Society before they closed and had just picked up the first can of dog food I saw at Pete's Market. Maybe I should have bought an assortment of flavors.

I was about to tell my new companion that I'd get him a flavor he liked, when he looked up at me and said, "*Muchas gracias.*"

"*De nada,*" I replied as he began gobbling up the food like he hadn't eaten for a week.

Wait a minute . . . he couldn't have spoken to me. And in Spanish, no less. I'd been alone too long. That was it. I was under a lot of stress. I was late with my homeowner's dues and late with my mortgage payments. I had started looking for work on Craigslist, but so far I wasn't making much progress. Thirty resumes out, but only one interview. That interview was with the owner of a private detective agency. Jimmy Gerrard had a sleazy appearance, a shabby office, and a weird way of talking about himself in the third person. Still, I was desperate and had tried to convince him I would make a good investigator. I have an eye for detail, I'm a good judge of character, and I speak a little Spanish.

The dog had emptied his food bowl and was licking his lips with his long pink tongue. He looked out toward the living room. *"Tu casa es hermosa, muy hermosa."*

"What?" I agreed that my home was pretty, but I didn't expect to hear it from him.

"Tu casa es mi casa," he said approvingly. He got it backwards, but I got the point: he felt at home.

He trotted into the living room and started looking around, more slowly this time. I poured myself a glass of Chardonnay and followed him. He seemed to like what he saw, his head bobbing up and down as he poked his nose into the corners. I sank down on my chocolate brown sofa and set my wineglass on the end table. Before I knew it, I had a Chihuahua in my lap. He proceeded to give my crotch a series of vigorous sniffs.

"Stop that," I scolded.

"I am a dog," he said. "What can I do?"

I was about to shoo him away, when he lay down in my lap and curled up, snug as a kitten. He was so soft and cuddly, his short fur like warm velvet. His long ears were shell pink where the light shone through them.

I mused aloud, "What shall we call you?"

"My name is Pepe," he answered in Spanish.

"Pepe?"

"Sí." He got off my lap and stood on the couch beside me, his huge brown eyes looking directly into mine. "And your name, senorita?" he continued, still speaking Spanish. "How are you called?"

"I'm Geri Sullivan," I told him.

"*Bueno*," he said, with a wagging tail. "I am now, with great pride, Pepe Sullivan."

I took another sip of my wine. This was too much.

Pepe looked me up and down. "You are *muy bonita*, Geri!"

I blinked. "Really?" It had been a long time since anyone had complimented me on my appearance.

"*Sí!* Your dark, curly hair gleams like the wing of a raven. Your lashes are as long and thick as a camel's. And your curves are as sultry as the Yucatan."

"Pepe," I said, "you are quite the flatterer." Although I was still pondering the comparison to a camel. Was that a compliment?

"I do not flatter," he said. "I speak only the truth. I can recognize a hot mama when I see one."

"Well, thank you," I said. They say dogs are man's best friend, but this one was definitely woman's best friend. He made me feel way better than any of the losers I had dated since the divorce.

"Geri," Pepe asked, "have you any other dogs?"

"No, I don't," I said. For some reason, I was reluctant to tell him about Albert. Just as I was reluctant to let Albert know about the dog.

"*Buenísimo!*" He nodded approvingly. "That makes me *el jefe*."

I didn't think Albert would agree with that and was about to tell him so, when my cell phone rang. I got up and fished it out of my brown leather purse.

I expected it to be my best friend and business partner, Brad. I had promised to stop by his shop to show him my new pet. So I was shocked when the caller introduced himself as Jimmy Gerrard, the owner of the Gerrard Agency.

"Jimmy G has good news!" he said. "You're hired."

It had been three weeks since the interview. I had long since given up hope that he would hire me. So it took me a moment to recover. "Great! When do I start?"

"Right now!"

"What do you mean *right now?*"

"Jimmy G means what he says. Right now. We've got a case!"

"OK," I said. I really wanted to spend my time getting the dog settled but I couldn't afford to pass up this opportunity. "Do you want me to meet you at the office?"

"You're on your own for this one," he said. "Jimmy G is in Portland. On another case. Tailing a suspect. But we got a call from a woman who lives on Capitol Hill. Her husband is missing, and Jimmy G needs someone to get over there to interview her. She's expecting you. Told her you could be there by four p.m."

I looked at the clock. It was 3:30. "But I've never done this before," I said. "I have no idea what to do—"

He cut me off. "You'll be fine. Find out what she wants. Take some shorthand." I wanted to tell him shorthand went out in the fifties, but he kept on going. "We can go over your notes when Jimmy G returns."

Pepe was still standing on the sofa, listening to me as I spoke on the phone. After I hung up, I turned to him and said, "That was good news, Pepe. I've got a job. I'm a private investigator, and I'm going out to interview a client." It seemed OK to brag a little, especially to a dog.

"I will go with you," he said.

"No, you have to stay here," I said as I slid my cell phone back into my purse.

"Por favor?"

I shook my head. "I'm not going to blow this chance just because I'm hallucinating a talking dog. You are a figment of my imagination."

"I am no figment," Pepe told me. "I am flesh and fur and blood. Am I not standing here before you?"

"Yes, but—"

"Oh, so you bring me home only to deny me." He turned away and walked to the other end of the couch, where he stopped, his head hanging low. "I am offended."

Poor guy. I went over and stroked his smooth back. "Pepe," I said, "I'm sorry. But it could be dangerous." I didn't really think so, but it made my life seem more glamorous. Although I wasn't sure why I was trying to impress my dog. But don't we all want to impress our dogs?

Pepe perked right up. "Dangerous, eh? I could be of help."

"You're just a little Chihuahua."

"I am full of machismo."

I smiled. "That's all well and good, but—"

"Trouble is my middle name," he told me. "Do you know that I have faced the bulls in Mexico City?"

"No."

"*Sí.*" He paused. "Well, truth be told, I only by accident fell into the bull ring—but I dodged *el toro* better than the matador. The entire crowd cheered for me."

"Really?"

"*Sí.* Now can I go with you?"

"No, Pepe. You have to stay here." I headed for the door. But I hadn't gone more than a few steps, when Pepe scampered after me.

"I have also worked as a search and rescue dog in Mexico City."

"You?"

"It takes a small dog to search small spaces after an earthquake. Tight places, dark places, dangerous spaces. But I am very brave."

"That's fine, but—"

"So now can I go?"

"I'm sorry," I told him. "I'll be right back. I'll only be gone about an hour."

He planted himself in front of the door.

"Additionally," he said, "I have worked with the federal authorities in the battle against the Mexican drug lords."

"Cut it out, Pepe. How could you have done all that? How old are you anyway?"

"Old enough to have done these things, and many more," he said.

I shook my head.

"You doubt me? I will show you. I have a good nose."

He headed for the living room and went straight to the black lacquered Chinese cabinet underneath my TV. I followed him.

"Here," he said, standing on his hind legs and scratching at the dangling gold tassel on the cabinet doors with his tiny pink paws. "Drugs."

I was stunned. "There aren't any drugs in there."

"No?" He sniffed at the drawer, his nose quivering. "I beg to differ. *Sí.* It is marijuana for certain."

"Oh, all right. But it isn't mine."

"Whatever."

"Really. Jeff must have left it behind—"

"So," Pepe interrupted, "I have proven myself. Now you must take me along."

"Fine, fine," I said. "I give up. I'll go get the leash."

"No leash."

"There's a leash law, Pepe, we—"

"How can I protect you if I am all tied up?" he asked. "Do not worry. I promise to walk only at your side. To heel, as it is called."

"OK, OK," I said. "But we have to go right now or we'll be late."

"*Sí. Vámonos,*" he said, leading the way to the door. "But I have to do one thing before we get into the car."

"What's that?" I said, as we went outside.

"I need to mark my territory."

Chapter 2

A cold, wet breeze was blowing from the south as we approached my green Toyota sedan, which was parked on the street. The day, like most April days in Seattle, had been fickle: rain showers alternating with sun breaks. But now a huge, black cloud hovered over the gray waters of nearby Lake Union, promising to fulfill the weatherman's prediction of a cold and stormy night.

"Are you sure we are in Seattle?" Pepe asked, as he sniffed at a dozen different spots on the grass of the parking strip. "It feels more like Nome, Alaska," he added with an extended shiver.

"I suppose I should get you a rain coat," I told him, fishing my car keys out of my purse. It was one of the things I was anticipating with pleasure. Chihuahuas look so cute when they are dressed up.

"No." His tone was authoritative.

"Why not?"

"Real dogs do not wear coats." With that, still

shivering, he went to my car's rear, curbside tire, lifted his hind leg and peed all over the hubcap.

"Pepe! Stop that!"

"I had to mark my territory," he said, walking up to me.

"Fine," I said. "But you didn't have to do it on my tire."

"It is the very best place, Geri."

"Why is that?"

"It is a little trick I picked up from my cousin, Chico," he explained. "If you park your car near our hacienda, all the senoritas in the neighborhood will soon know that I live here. But your car, it also gets around—this means that senoritas all over town will know of Pepe el Macho. It is simple."

I couldn't argue with his logic, but I told him, "Don't do it again."

"If it makes you unhappy, I will not do it anymore. I solemnly promise." He said this with an overblown sincerity that made me nervous. "Now can we get in the car already?" he asked, shivering mightily. "I am freezing my tail off."

I opened the rear passenger door for him, but he didn't budge.

"I ride only in the front," he said.

I didn't have time to argue with him.

I closed the rear door and opened the front one. "OK, you win. Just get in," I told him, then remembered how short he was. "Here," I added, bending down, "I'll help you."

"I can do it myself." With a mighty leap he launched

himself from the pavement to the floorboard of the car, and from there another jump took him to the passenger seat.

I got in and started the engine. As I put on my seatbelt, I looked over at my canine passenger and had to say that he looked quite handsome. He sat up straight, his head lifted, though I doubted he could see over the dashboard.

"Well," I asked him. "Ready to go?"

"*Sí*," he answered. "But there is just one thing."

"What's that?"

"Crack open my window a bit, *por favor*," he said. "I get carsick."

The woman I was supposed to interview, Rebecca Tyler, lived on Fourteenth Avenue East, a street also known as Millionaire's Row, because it's lined with huge, turn-of-the-century mansions built by Seattle's early merchants and timber barons. It was a wide, stately street, lined with tall elms and horse chestnut trees. The houses were set back behind manicured lawns and wrought-iron fences, all well preserved in styles of the past: Southern colonial, Tudor revival, neoclassical. The people who built them had big money back then; the people living in them now had big money today.

I didn't know much about my client, just that her husband was missing and instead of calling the police she had called Jimmy Gerrard. Perhaps her husband had run off with another woman, and she didn't want to expose herself to the public scrutiny a police investigation would involve.

As we pulled up in front of the Tyler residence, Pepe, who had been talking non-stop the whole way there, said, "Are we here? Is this the place?"

"I think so." I took out my notes to double-check the address.

Pepe stood, putting his forelegs on the armrest so he could see out the window. "The house number—what is it?"

"It's 640," I told him. The house sat behind a wrought-iron fence with pointed barbs. Huge stone pillars flanked the driveway with the house number displayed in tile on either side.

"*Sí,*" Pepe told me. "*Seis cuatro cero.* This is the correct *casa.*"

Casa seemed a misnomer, I thought. It wasn't just the biggest home on the block, it was a gigantic white wedding cake of a mansion. Four huge white Corinthian columns on either side of the entryway supported a gracefully curved upper deck. Gold-painted lion statues guarded the wide stairs leading up to the front door.

"I do not like those big lions," said Pepe.

"They're not real."

"Still, they give me a sense of unease."

"Fine. Just be quiet for a minute," I told him. "I want to make sure I'm prepared." I grabbed my big brown leather purse and rooted around to find my pen.

"You tell me to be silent? I am insulted."

"Look, Pepe, your mouth hasn't stopped during this whole trip. You talk more than any dog I ever knew." I stopped, realizing how absurd that sounded.

He hung his head. "Perhaps it is because you are the only person who has ever listened to me in my whole life."

That stung me—I certainly knew what it was like when nobody would listen to you. I gave him a gentle pat on the head.

"I apologize," I told my tough little *hombre* with the delicate feelings.

He perked right up, his tail wagging. "Then I can talk?"

"Yes, you can talk."

"Look there, Geri," he said, looking out at the house again. "The front door—it is ajar. Is that not strange?"

"Yes, it is," I said. I watched the door for a minute, but saw no sign of activity. "You stay here." I opened the car door. "I'm going to check it out."

"Me, too." Before I knew it, Pepe had scrambled across my lap and out of the car. He ran up the stairs and into the house in a flash.

"Pepe!"

Chapter 3

How could such a tiny dog run so fast? And how would I explain his presence to the client? I scrambled to catch up with him.

I paused at the open front door and caught my breath, hoping Pepe would appear in the entryway. The foyer was all white marble and crystal chandeliers, with a huge semicircular staircase as the centerpiece. I rang the doorbell, which produced a mournful series of chimes but no human response. I didn't know if I could just walk in. What were the rules about that?

I rang the doorbell again. Still no answer. But this time I did hear a faint and distant yip coming from somewhere to the right. It was the first time I'd ever heard Pepe bark. Although it didn't really sound like a bark. More like the sound a tiny Chihuahua might make right before being gobbled up by a tough pit bull.

That thought got me moving. I dashed through

the foyer and headed right, finding myself in an all-white living room, one of the largest I had ever seen. The carpet was a snowy white, the walls were papered in white damask, the curtains were clouds of white satin. Even the grand piano in the corner was white. It desperately needed a spot of color, something like the bright red throw rug under the glass coffee table.

It took a second before it sank in. That wasn't a rug, but a pool of blood. As I got closer, I saw that it surrounded the body of a man who lay face down on the white carpet. Pepe was sniffing the bottoms of his shoes. The man wore Birkenstocks, those clunky sandals so popular in Seattle, over green socks.

Pepe lifted his head. "You should not be here," he said. "We must leave right now." He headed toward me, leaving a trail of tiny red footprints behind him.

"No, we can't leave!" I said, darting toward the prone figure. I bent over and put my fingers against his neck. "What if he's still alive?"

"Believe me, he is *muy muerto!*" Pepe said. He was right. The man's skin was gray and felt cool beneath my fingertips.

I willed myself to study the corpse. He had sandy-colored hair pulled back into a short ponytail at the base of his neck. He wore a pair of khaki pants and a yellow T-shirt with some sort of lettering on it, hard to read now because it was mottled with brown stains.

"Who is he?" I asked.

"I do not know," said Pepe. "All I know is we must get out of here! Something stinks about this situation, and it is not just the smell of death." He wrinkled his nose expressively.

A gun lay a few inches from the man's right hand. "This must be the murder weapon," I said, picking it up.

"Do not touch that!" said Pepe. "Do you not know anything about crime-scene investigation?"

Too late. It was already in my hand.

"How do you know about crime-scene investigation?" I asked, turning the gun over to examine it.

"I am a big fan of TV crime shows," he said. "*CSI. Forensic Files.* I watch them all. *CSI: Miami* is the best. Now put that down!"

But before I could put it back, somebody behind me yelled, "Drop it, lady!"

"Set it down nice and slow," another voice commanded.

I turned and saw two uniformed policemen. Both had pistols trained on me.

"I said drop it!"

Without even thinking, I did as they said. The gun slid from my grasp and fell onto the glass coffee table, which shattered into a million pieces.

"*Policía* . . ." I heard Pepe mutter as he slunk underneath the sofa.

In no time, the police had put me in handcuffs. They had taken a quick look at the corpse and then called for backup. Soon the room was full of policemen, four or five in blue uniforms, two in suits, and three or four in white jumpsuits and blue paper booties. A pair of detectives (the ones in suits) took me into the dining room, which was just as huge as the living room, but all done up in gold, from the gilded coffered ceiling to the bronze satin on the chair seats. I shuddered to think about the rest of the color scheme in the house. I was willing to bet there was a bathroom done all in shades of purple.

One of the men looked a bit like my father, with his wire-rim glasses and thinning brown hair combed over a bald spot. He wore a rumpled navy suit. The other one was a handsome black man with a shiny, shaved head. His suit was gray, paired with a blue silk shirt and silver cufflinks. The older man said his name was Detective Earl Larson; the other guy was Detective Kevin Sanders.

"Did you find Mrs. Tyler?" I asked. It occurred to me that she might be somewhere in the house, perhaps in one of the upper rooms, as dead as her husband. (I had learned from overhearing snippets of conversation that the body in the living room belonged to David Tyler.) But the police had fanned out and searched the house and grounds without finding any other bodies or any trace of Rebecca Tyler. "She was supposed to be here."

"Why were you meeting her?" Larson wanted to know.

"I'm a private investigator," I said. I didn't want

to say more. I knew from reading detective novels that PIs had the right to keep their conversations with their clients private, just like priests and lawyers.

Larson asked to see my license.

"I don't have one yet," I explained. "I was just hired. This is my first assignment."

"Who's your boss?"

"Jimmy Gerrard of the Gerrard Agency."

"Why isn't he here?"

"He's in Portland right now, working on another case." I thought it sounded good that he had trusted me with such an important assignment. But Larson shook his head. I could tell he didn't believe me.

"We're going to have to take you down to the precinct for questioning," he said. Sanders motioned for me to get up, and they walked me towards the front door, one on each side as if they were afraid I was going to make a dash for it.

"I'm not leaving without my dog," I said. I hadn't seen Pepe since the police had first burst into the room.

"What dog?" Sanders asked.

"He's a little white Chihuahua," I said. "He was in the living room with me. Maybe you missed him because he's the same color as the room." That was supposed to be a joke but apparently they didn't think it was funny. It's one of my faults, at least according to my ex, that I tend to make jokes when they're not appropriate.

Sanders went into the living room and talked to some of the other men there. A man with a large camera was wandering around, taking photos of the shattered coffee table and the gun.

One of the guys in the white jumpsuits pulled aside one of the white satin curtains and came up with a small white object. He held it in front of him with gloved hands, as if it were contaminated.

It was Pepe! I could tell he wasn't happy. He pedaled his feet in the air, as if trying to find firm ground.

"That's my dog!" I said, rushing towards him. But Larson blocked my way.

The photographer stepped forward and snapped a photo. The flash went off in Pepe's face and he flinched.

"You can't touch him, ma'am," the technician said. "He's evidence." He pointed to Pepe's paws, which were caked with blood. "We're going to have to take him to the lab to be processed."

"No way, José!" I heard Pepe mutter. He squirmed around and bit the technician on the wrist. The man dropped him with a cry of pain, and Pepe hit the floor, making his own little yelp as he landed. Then he dashed between Larson's legs and darted out through the open front door.